Stone Dragon

Also by Klay Testamark

Iron Elf
Wyvern Hunters (novella)

Stone Dragon

Book 1 of the First Realm Saga

Klay Testamark

© 2013 Klay Testamark
ISBN: 0615866433
ISBN-13: 978-0615866437

Dedication

This book is for Lisa, Ally, and Glen II. My loving family, who supported me in more ways than I can count.

Acknowledgements

I'd like to thank the following people for their assistance with this book: editor Joe Galindez, illustrator Carlos Herrera, designer Megan McCullough, proofreader Sarah Madison, and beta readers Kevin Bailey, Steave Bailey, and Nicole Mehrman.

Table of Contents

Maps and Illustrations

Chapter 1

The king is dead!
Long live the king!
But
the new king is dead also
and him the last of the line
Madness rules the streets of Drystone
Who there is left to the throne of Brandish?
Who there is left to lead we elves?
Dark days approach
Our enemies grow strong
An heir must be found
An heir there shall be

Know him you will
by his silver hand
Ignorant of his past
Ignorant of his future
He will deny his fate he will run from his fate
knowing not that all roads lead to destiny
Friend to humans
Friend to dwarves
Friend even to halflings
He is kin to dragons
this heir
The last of those great beasts shall bow to him
shall be as a brother to him
Look you well upon this prince!
Last of a majestic line!
First of a new order
Nothing is the same again.

This is how it ends. Two friends in the dungeons and two friends fighting on the wall. And me, bleeding to death in the courtyard while my enemies hovered close.

I cannot move. I cannot fight. I can only reflect on the chain of events that brought me to this point.
It isn't easy being an elf.

"It isn't easy being an elf," I said. My companions at the table looked at me in surprise. They were three dwarfs and a human woman.

"What makes you say that?" said Jodo, one of the dwarfs. "You're a city elf. You don't have to mine your own ore—"

"—or hunt your own food—"

"—or use magic items. You *are* magic."

I looked at them. "That's a bit unsettling."

"When you're out in the wilderness with no one else to talk to—"

"—except your two brothers—"

"—well, can you blame us?"

"Okay, so it's not easy being a dwarf either." I turned to the woman. Sandahl probably outweighed me by fifty pounds, but she had a pretty face and a chest you could rest your glass on. I gave her my most charming smile and said, "Surely you can see that an elf's life is a hard one?"

"I don't know," she said. "Do you deal with chilly summers and dark crushing winters?"

"No."

"Do you live with constant tribal warfare?"

"No."

"Then what's your problem?"

"It is a most vexing one," I said. "Elves live too long."

Silence.

"Oh, this is getting interesting!" said Lodo, the last dwarf. "How is that a problem?"

"It gives us too much time."

"Don't let a halfling hear that," Sandahl said. "They don't have a tenth as much as you do."

"And look at them!" I said. "They pack so much experience into a few short decades. A halfling can become a hero, establish a kingdom, and die a great-grandfather, all in less than a century. Dynasties can rise and fall in the time it takes for an elf to reach adulthood."

"I've always thought a long childhood was a good thing," said Kodo, the second dwarf. He drank from his tankard. "We dwarves may not live a full thousand years, but we do okay."

"What is it—seven, eight hundred years?" I said. I turned to Sandahl. "Humans can live that long, right?"

"Rarely," she said.

"Why not?" Jodo said. "You've got that healing factor going for you. Come to think of it, I've never seen an old human."

"We're not big believers in dying of old age," she said. "It used to be that when a warrior grew tired of life he would seek out a dragon and do his best to kill it."

"What happened?" I asked.

"The dragon usually won, but then the warrior's clan would declare vendetta on it. Dragon or not, few things can survive that."

"I should think so," I said. "There's just one human here and I can't resist her."

She giggled.

"Is that why there aren't dragons anymore?" Lodo asked. "Humans killed them off?"

"Maybe in the Northlands," I said. "That doesn't explain why they've disappeared from the continent. Until elves came to power, they used to be all over Brandish."

"So elves killed them off?"

"No," I said. "We dealt with them on a case-to-case basis. Maybe it was dwarves."

"Us? Inconceivable!" Jodo said, thumping the table. "We are a peaceful folk. Who ever heard of dwarves going up against a dragon?"

"They were always a, y'know, dying breed," Kodo said. "Lived for tens of thousands of years but rarely reproduced. Wouldn't take much to push a species like that to extinction."

Everyone looked at me.

"What?"

"So you're saying the problem with elves is they don't get enough in the bedroom?" Jodo asked.

"NO!" I said. "That's not it at all!"

"I've always wondered," Sandahl said. "I mean, elves stay youthful up until the end, right? And you all look so pretty." Here she pinched my cheek. "So why isn't the world filled with pointy-eared babies? Do elves have a low sex drive?"

"I assure you, madam, my drive is as high as any human's."

She laughed. I pressed on: "What I'm saying is that, since elves live so long, they're seldom in any kind of hurry. And that's boring." I took a drink. "Elves are a shade quicker and a bit more magic. We don't suddenly go through puberty and we don't suffer from rampant fertility—but listen, it's not for me to say which race is better. There is no *better*."

The last line was a bit slurred. I may or may not have drunk too much. I continued:

"The mouse and the elephant count the same number of heartbeats. A billion and a half beats for both. Subjectively, the elephant lives longer than the mouse —about as long as a halfling—but it seems the mouse lives more intensely. I've certainly never seen one look bored."

"Are you calling us mice?" Jodo asked. He'd been drinking all night as well.

"I don't know. Run after any farmer's wives?"

"Why you..." said Lodo.

"I am not calling you mice. That would make me the elephant, and I haven't the nose for it. Anyway, a sword is better than another sword if it holds its edge longer. A bow is better than another if it draws more smoothly. But a thinking being and another thinking being? How is one better? For what purpose? You can't judge us as if we were tools."

"Tha's funny," said Sandahl. "Because I'd be interested in judging your—"

"Elves, dwarves, and humans are obviously related!" said Kodo, who was an indignant drunk. "Why are we so differn't, then?"

"We're not," I said. "Were I a taxonomist I would put the three of you much closer to my family tree than, say, the chimpanzee."

All three dwarves lunged. Since we had a table between us, they mostly knocked the wind out of themselves. Jodo managed to draw his axe, but even in my inebriated state I successfully took it away from him. Sandahl pushed them back into their chairs and I tried to calm everyone down.

"Here is your axe back, my good man. You shouldn't take offense at what I say. After all, aren't we practically brothers? And since I am once again paying for this round, please be so kind as to let me finish."

I took a drink and continued. "First there's the long childhood, which is more tedious than you'd think. Then, by the time you're ready to enter society, they've indoctrinated you so thoroughly that you can't be anything but a model elf. And even when you're considered an adult, all of the important people in society still have *centuries* left to live. Is it any wonder that nothing changes here? Being an elf is boring because nobody's allowed to be an amateur at anything."

If you've never seen a drunken elf, you haven't lived. Then again, if you've ever seen a drunken elf, I congratulate you for having survived. We are by nature a passionate race. It's one reason we have such long childhoods, to train it out of us. However, all that training goes out the window when we reach age fifty and can finally go to the alehouse. An elf's first drink is a day to be remembered. Maybe not by him personally, but certainly by everyone else.

You can always tell a birthday party by the broken glass on the floor and the scorch marks on the ceiling.

The rest of the night passed uneventfully. My friends and I drank until the dead of the morning. Sandahl and I then took the dwarves home. I staggered along with Jodo, and Sandahl more or less carried his two brothers. Home, in their case, was a rented room in the Old Quarter. Small, but inexpensive and clean.

Afterward the human woman and I found another inn and… well, let's just say we weren't too drunk.

Later I found myself walking to the alehouse. It was still some time before sunrise and the fog had not yet lifted. It hung all around and made distant lighthouses out of the street lamps. My boots rang upon the cobbles. The sound was large in the empty city.

The lamps must have guttered, because the lights flickered. I blinked. It seemed like a warning.

I became aware of another set of footsteps. They were clear and loud, so I looked about. "Hello?"

Nothing. Just the sound of another walker beating pavement, matching me step for step.

I stopped and readied a defensive spell, while reaching mentally into hammerspace in case I needed weapons. "Okay, this isn't funny."

The footsteps were closer now—I settled into a fighting stance and prepared to face the enemy.

An elf came out of the mist. He was tall, and blonde, and familiar.

"Dinendal?" I said. I blinked. "Is that you?"

He looked so much like my best friend. He even had Dinny's trademark smirk. He came within ten feet and went past, vanishing into the fog.

"Dinendal!" I hurried after, but he was gone. Had he ducked into an alley? Why hadn't he spoken?

I was breathing hard. I leaned against a lamppost to catch my breath. Maybe I was drunker than I thought.

Elrond's Commonwealth served breakfast, but I was more in need of a hangover cure. Of course, as Elrond the bartender pointed out, I wouldn't even have a hangover if I'd stuck to elven wines.

"Maybe I like the variety," I said. "Come on, Elrond! More wine!"

"Master Angrod, you're a wizard's apprentice. A *graduating* apprentice. You know at least four hangover cures far more effective than hair of the dog."

I squinted at him. "Glass," I said, raising it. "Empty. This is a problem."

"Haven't you had enough? The weekend is over. Don't you have errands?"

"They'll still be there when I'm done," I said. I rummaged in hammerspace until I found the scrap of paper: *Go to the beach. Get 9 buckets black sand and 2 buckets white sand. White sand from a cave on the northern shore.*

"It can wait," I said. I reached for the bottle in Elrond's hands, but he pulled it away. "First tell me what the four cures are," he said.

"Fine, *professor*." I sat up as if I were in a classroom. "I could use water magic to ease the symptoms or fire magic to speed up my metabolism. I could use air magic to function at a normal level, despite the headache, or I could use earth magic to simply ignore the hangover."

"Very good. And what can a skilled wizard do?"

"A skilled wizard can blend all of the different cures until the hangover is completely gone. Do I get a gold star?"

"No, but you get a drink," he said, and filled my glass. "Drink up, now. I'm sure your master told you not to dawdle."

"Valandil said, *Don't take forever this time, lad, I have to finish the wall for the council.* Lad! If I were a halfling I'd be a village elder now."

"But you're not a halfling, be thankful."

"I'll be thankful after this drink," I said. I took a swallow. "An apprentice has rights, you know. He has me doing things like a common servant and he knows I'd rather be working for the city. I'm a decent mage and I know the nine weapons. I could join the watch or the royal guard, or even run missions for the council."

Elrond was polishing a glass, as bartenders are wont to do. "I see it differently. Master Valandil has been teaching you about humility through these meaningless tasks. You know what he says: *Before wisdom, chop wood and carry water.*"

"After wisdom, chop wood and carry water," I finished. "Crazy old man. Wonder if he got it off a postcard."

"Master Angrod, you will soon be a journeyman, with the right to choose your own path—whether it is to adventure with the wood elves or return to a noble's life in the north. In the meantime, respecting your mentor is the least you could be doing."

I slammed my glass down. "Collecting sand to transmogrify is *not* what I wanted to be doing. Elrond, I haven't seen my home since my aunt died. In forty-five years I have not felt proper snow beneath my feet or breathed air that didn't stink of fish. I miss my best friend Dinendal. Do you know, I think I saw him on the way here. But it couldn't have been him."

"Mm-hmm," he said. He went to the back room and came out with something, which he placed on the bar. "Here you go."

I stared. "What's that?"

"The mulberry wine your master ordered. Don't you remember why you came in last night?"

I looked at the list. On the other side was, *1 small keg Elrond's finest.* "Oh yes. I told him it was my treat."

Elrond's Commonwealth was one of the finest alehouses in Drystone, but Elrond was also famous for his mulberry, blueberry, and gooseberry wines. Small wonder, since he had been royal winemaker when the city had a king. That was nine hundred years ago, but it was still his privilege to take the best berries from the royal garden.

That place, like the royal palace, was lovingly maintained. I wondered briefly about a city that would behead its ruler and topple his statues, yet keep his house and tend his berry orchards.

I looked at the barrel of wine. Elrond made the best wine in the city, but—

"It's got corners," I said.

"Have you never seen a square barrel before?"

"I… but… *why?*"

He rubbed his hands. "I have a nephew who's just full of ideas. Made it out of oak staves, gives the wine more contact with the wood. Gives it a nice spicy flavour too. What's more, the little spigot makes it so convenient. There's a deposit, by the way."

"Wine in a box?" I said. "It'll never catch on."

"Nevertheless."

I had an existential moment, which often happens at Elrond's. "Can't argue with elves, even if you are one yourself," I said. "Is it strong and sweet? He likes his wine after dinner, and I need him in a generous mood."

"Yes," he said. "And yes. You know, if you weren't a noble you probably couldn't afford all that wine."

"If I weren't a noble, I'd be home," I said. "And there's the tragedy."

"Are you planning something? The last time you bought Master Valandil wine, you went hunting for wyverns. You were banned from leaving the city after he found out." He leaned close and smiled his bartender's smile, which declared, *You can trust me.*

I'm brother to all drinking beings. "You're planning something, aren't you?"

"Now, now," I said, picking up the keg. "The past week was murder—each and every one of the masters tested me hard."

"That can't have been so bad. I've heard you're one of the best apprentices. What is it now? Running away to live with the humans? Or going off to the forest to see naked wood elves?"

"It's nearly dawn," I said hoisting the keg onto my shoulder. "I can only hope today will be better. Although knowing Valandil, he'll have me assisting him all day. To the crows with architecture!" I spun on my heel and walked to the door.

—only to have the door swing wide. It hit me in the nose and knocked the wine out of my hand.

Chapter 2

S everal things happened at once.

I stumbled back—the box wine fell—Elrond yelled, *"The wine!"*—and a glyph appeared before my eyes and I poured energy into it.

Featherfall isn't a particularly elegant spell. It simply grabs all the air in the vicinity and forces it under whatever's falling. It's like hitting a warm feather bed, and for that reason it's one of the first things taught to elven children. Later on, when they're old enough for weapons training, it's also the first thing drilled into them. Elves hate accidents, and especially dying of accidents.

My ears popped. The windows blew in. Every bottle behind the counter went *bang!* I winced. Featherfall isn't for indoor use. In fact, it's why elven training halls have big open windows.

The box wine slowed, sank, and hit the floor with gentlest of thumps.

I became aware that I was holding my fighting sticks. The carvings glowed because I'd teleported them into my hands. My hands were already weaving back and forth.

My opponent squared off in front of me. Her feet were set wide. She held fists out in a rigid guard. She was dressed from head to toe in black leather. It moulded to her body in stiff plates.

"Come on if you think you're hard enough!" I heard myself say.

"*Angrod Veneanar and Meerwen Elanesse!* Stop this at once!"

I froze. That didn't sound like my friendly neighbourhood bartender! I looked back and saw Elrond dripping expensive wine.

"Before you kill each other, I'd like to know which of you is going to pay for this."

"I will," my opponent and I said at the same time.

I looked at her. She'd oiled her black hair and sculpted it into a sort of helmet, but what I saw of her face was extremely pleasant. And all that leather left little to the imagination.

There was something else, too. Call it déjà vu. Call it recognition for someone you've never met. The entire world leaped an inch to the left—my heart included. I looked into her eyes and almost fell in.

I wanted to ask if she was feeling the same. Instead I said, "I do apologize, but it was my spell, and I ought to pay."

"And I apologize also. I should have opened the door more gently. And I am more than capable of paying my way."

"Your pardon, but I am Angrod, apprentice to Master Valandil and youngest son of House Veneanar. I shouldn't trouble you with the expense."

"I beg your pardon also, but I am Meerwen, daughter of Lord Governor Findecano Elanesse, and I am not troubled at all." I saw that she also wore a cape of sea green, the colour of the upstart House Elanesse.

We saluted each other. I crossed my forearms in front of me and bowed my head over them. Being unarmed, she simply struck her right fist to her chest and bowed her head. My heels touched. Hers clicked.

"I'll put it on both your tabs, how's that sound?" Elrond said, towelling himself off with a counter rag. A clean one, I hoped.

"Tell you what," he said. "Since it was an accident I'll give you both a discount."

"You've never given a discount before," I said, making my sticks disappear. "This calls for a drink!"

"Sure, why not." He brought out a glass and wrung the bar rag over it.

Meerwen stared. "Er, maybe another time," she said. "And it's really no trouble to pay for everything."

Elrond chuckled. "This sort of thing happens every time somebody has a birthday. I buy cheap booze from a halfling peddler and re-bottle it. Don't worry."

"That's a relief," I said.

"What can I do for you, young lady?" Elrond said.

Meerwen walked past. "Do you have the gooseberry wine? Father is having a few guests tonight."

Elrond smiled. "I have it right here. He'll love this vintage—and his guest will be sure to remark at the packaging." He disappeared into the back room.

"Packaging?" Meerwen said.

"You'll see," I said, picking up my box wine. "You know, I'm glad we met. I rarely run into women of such beauty."

"And not quite so hard, I hope?" She was smiling.

"You have the better of me," I said, and bowed. "I have the feeling we've met before, but I'm sure I would've remembered such a lovely face."

"You needn't impress me with fine compliments, Angrod Veneanar. Sorry about the door."

"It's nothing, Meerwen Elanesse. You know, my friends call me—"

"Angie?"

I spluttered. "Roddy, actually."

There were footsteps. "—this is the best-tasting gooseberry wine in all of Drystone, I stake my reputation on it," Elrond said, coming out with another little barrel."

"It's got corners," Meerwen said.

"Don't ask," I said.

She turned to leave. "Well, Angrod, it's been an interesting meeting."

I bowed again. "I look forward to our next one and truly hope it is much longer."

"And without doors, I'm sure," she said, and left.

Elrond and I watched her leave. Oddly enough, the hang of her cape didn't keep me from enjoying the view.

"That's quite a woman," I said. Absently I picked a glass off the table and took a sip. "*Pfaugh!* That's awful!"

"I know," Elrond said. "They say if you drink enough you start talking to giant weasels. Keep drinking and they start talking back. I'm not sure you should be trying to impress that girl. She *is* the daughter of the most powerful man in the First Realm."

"Damn, I forgot. The Lord Governor of Drystone wouldn't take too kindly to me as Meerwen's boyfriend, would he?"

"I shouldn't think so, no."

"I've been in this city a long time. Why haven't I seen her?"

"She's just recently returned from the convent."

"She's a *nun?*"

"The Fighting Nuns also train lay persons. They say when fist meets face, anyone can die." He took out a broom and began sweeping up the broken glass. "Don't you have a job to do? Other places to be?"

"I'll be going," I said. "Hey, in the interest of never tasting it again, what was that wretched wine?"

Elrond shrugged. "It goes by many names, but the most popular is *El Vagabundo*."

I went straight to Valandil's home before heading for the beach. It wouldn't take a moment to gather the white sand, but there was no telling how long to find the cave. After setting the wine on the kitchen table I stepped into the courtyard and teleported to the beach.

Teleport is one of the first spells an elf learns upon beginning a wizard's apprenticeship, assuming he has a talent for it. Considering all the assignments a master is wont to give, it's not hard to guess why. I've often wondered whether the chores came about because apprentices could teleport, or whether the spell came about *because* masters gave so many chores. Either way, it gets lots of practice.

Carrying a shovel and a stack of wooden buckets, I cleared my mind, closed my eyes, and jumped into the air. As the ground dropped away, I concentrated on the beach, while trying hard to forget about the courtyard. For a crucial second I believed I was at the beach and that my feet would land on midnight-black sand.

My boots hit the ground with a crunch. I opened my eyes and saw the ocean.

The wind blew strongly landward, carrying spray in from the sea. The ocean looked restless and full of secrets, but that was probably just the tail end of last night's drinking. There seemed to be a storm coming.

I set the buckets down and filled nine of them with black sand. Then I slipped them into hammerspace and looked for white sand.

Hammerspace is why elf clothing doesn't have many pockets. Think of it as your own personal twilight zone. Have you ever lost something, only to find it hours later, even though you'd checked that pocket? Did you think you didn't search enough? Elves know the truth. Pockets aren't hard to search. It's just that stuff drops out of existence sometimes.

Being a practical folk, we've harnessed this phenomenon. It's easy: Take something in hand, slip it out of sight, and forget you're holding it. We don't know where it goes, but it keeps well. We've learned a few other things. For instance, the elsewhere place can only carry items you can hold in one hand, and only you can retrieve what you put away. Rabbits and doves can be stored with no ill effect, even for months. Food won't go bad and ice won't even melt, which might mean that time doesn't flow in there.

... The wind was cold, so I twirled the shovel and tossed it from hand to hand to stay loose...

Hammerspace seems to have unlimited capacity, but it's unpredictable. Things with moving parts often come back disassembled, even combined with other objects. Knives tend to return without their sheaths, their blades absurdly sharp. And from time to time objects will disappear completely, perhaps to a hammerspace *within* hammerspace.

Despite those quirks, the pocket dimension is tremendously useful. For safety and easy recall elves keep only a few things in there, about as much as a large purse could hold. We learn to use hammerspace from a young age—children keep their toys in it, which is how it gets its name, elf girls having a nasty sense of humour.

I saw no one else as I walked. It was easy to see why: the sky was overcast and the wind was turning wild. It was the wet season, and every elf knows not to stand on a beach during a thunderstorm.

White surf on black sand made for a nice contrast. A long time ago the sand had been volcanic rock. Now it was flecked with lighter grains. They glittered in the early-morning sun.

The black sand was plentiful and easily gathered, even by unskilled labourers, so it took care of most of Drystone's construction needs. White sand, meanwhile, was only for ornamentation. It made some beautiful detail work but only Valandil had a ready supply. It was one reason he was in such demand as a builder.

He'd always gotten the sand himself, and until today I'd never known where the source was. I had never expected him to tell me either. A master isn't required to share every secret with a soon-to-be competitor.

Did this mean he wanted me to take over the business? I shook my head and smiled. It was a sweet gesture, but I didn't see myself being a builder for the rest of my life.

I saw the cave. The current and the waves had carved a door into a wall of rock.

Chapter 3

There was a deep tide pool directly in front of it, so I teleported to the mouth of the cave.

Some wizards say teleporting isn't really teleporting. You're actually jumping into a parallel universe that's maybe ninety-nine percent identical to the original. It's not noticeably changed, but it *is* different. According to those wizards, you ought to say goodbye to your family the first time you teleport, because you're never seeing them again.

But then, it would be hard to get anything done without teleporting, so people do it anyway. Convenience wins over metaphysical doubt.

It grew dark as I made my way into the cave, so I snapped my fingers and produced a small flame. It hovered in front as I walked deeper underground.

I had gone some distance when the flame bumped into a dead end. It looked natural, but I recognized the style Valandil used when he was going for the organic look. I put down the buckets, raised my hands in front of me, and pressed them against the wall. A pulse went through my palms and down my arms. The rock wall dissolved. I shook my boots free of the resulting sand and stepped through.

It was a large cavern. The floor was white sand raked flat. There was also a camp bed, a couple of folding chairs, and a table. A glass, a box wine, and a lit gas lantern were on the table.

"Thanks for the mulberry wine," Valandil said. He sipped the wine from one of the chairs.

Imagine an elf—tall, lean, and high-shouldered, with a shaved skull, long green eyes, and a white braided moustache. Invest him with a dry intellect, no detectable sense of humour, and an endless capacity for assigning chores. Imagine that awful being and you have a picture of Valandil Telrunya, former royal advisor and my mentor.

"What are you doing here?" I asked. "I was about to return to the shop."

"I came over to talk. I've been waiting for you. Look, you'd better sit down."

I took the other chair rather nervously. While it was up to the other masters to decide if I'd passed my apprenticeship, I still needed Valandil's blessing to take on any work. I didn't see myself doing much building, but I wanted as many options as possible.

"Is this about my pub crawl? Because I didn't think you needed the sand until this afternoon."

He waved it away. "It's not that, although I was hoping to see you earlier. Do you know I used to advise King Galdor?"

"How could I forget? You advised him that heads were going out of style."

He coughed. "I told him to withdraw to a more secure location."

"In other words, run for cover?"

"A king never runs, he only advances in a different direction."

Here it comes. I started counting down.

Valandil looked like he was about to say something, but stopped. He sighed. "Things used to be better then."

Ask any elf over nine hundred and he'll usually tell you the past was so much nicer. People were less petty, children obeyed their elders, and musicians were respectable. Plays were deep and socially relevant, as well as funny as hell. It seems everything went into the midden once we started trying out this newfangled democracy.

There had been a revolution. Not a terribly violent one, but the king had been executed. Power had devolved to the governors of every city, and that's how it's been for nearly a millennium.

Galdor had been a decent king, but the council of governors had also done quite well. I'm not saying the government was any less corrupt, but at least we never elected leaders like King Myrdal the Mad, who had squandered the treasury on wars, and also drooled all the time.

"I don't see how they could be better," I said. "We've got peace, security, and brisk trade with the human kingdoms."

"Ugh," Valandil said, shaking his head. "A pack of starving dogs. If it weren't for the royal guard they'd have invaded long ago. That's right, the *royal* guard."

He began to lecture on all the things that used to be better when we had an off-with-his-head kind of leader. Humans and dwarves had looked up to elves, he said. They took our word seriously on every subject. No corner of the earth was ignorant of our flag. The way Valandil put it, elves had been covered in glory once, though to me that glory looked suspiciously like blood.

By this time I'd filled my own glass (Elrond was right, it *was* convenient) and settled in the other chair. I was into my second drink before he finally slowed down.

"… and another thing, the days used to be longer," he said, breathing hard.

I frowned. "I'm sure that's not something anybody can control. Not even a king."

"We shall soon see," he said. "Before long, Brandish shall once again be a kingdom."

"Impossible," I said. Errol Lissesul, the crown prince, had been abroad when his father died. He rushed home but died in a shipwreck. Having no children, siblings, or even cousins, this meant the royal line died with him.

"I've always wondered why Prince Errol came from a long line of only sons," I said. "Is it just me, or was House Lissesul terribly infertile? Even by elf standards it wasn't a big family."

"The Kings of Brandish have always allied themselves with queens of the highest breeding," Valandil said.

"So, inbred."

"I prefer the term *rarefied blood*."

"Rare is right. Not a drop is to be found these days."

"That's where you're wrong! For you see, my apprentice, I have reason to believe there are several quarts of it in this very cave."

I looked into my wine glass. Then I glanced around the chamber and settled back on Valandil. "A secret heir, in this place?" I said. "What's he been doing all this time?"

"Well, right now he's sipping mulberry wine."

I did a spit-take. "*You're* the heir to the throne?"

"No, you are, Angrod. I've searched a long time, and I believe it's you."

I wiped my mouth. "Very funny, sir. I know some masters like to play pranks on their apprentices, but I never imagined you'd be the type." I took a breath. "I'm House Veneanar! Strictly minor aristocracy! Ours is an ancient line, but our claim to the throne is no stronger than any other family's. By what complicated manner did I suddenly gain royal status?"

"If you'll let me finish," he said, "I will tell you."

If you can believe Valandil, the chambermaid did it.

They say you never really know anyone until you've been friends a couple of decades. I'm starting to believe this is true—I had no idea my mentor was a part-time genealogist.

There hadn't been a royal sex scandal since King Lavin the Loverboy (not as famous as King Fingol the Finger...biter) but Valandil reasoned that every prince had to have an affair or two, because who wouldn't?

I had to agree. If you have money, power, and a title, all you need to get women are working genitalia. Sometimes you don't even need those—witness King Cameron the Straperon.

Valandil interviewed every associate of Prince Errol's, hoping to uncover some secret assignation or drunken encounter. He sent letters to consuls, base commanders, and even former squires. Nothing. Errol had been no Prince Charming.

"No women in his life? How about men, then?"

Valandil grimaced. "If only. There is precedent for transferring title to the heirs of a same-sex lover—recall Princess Iminye—but the Crown Prince had no lovers of any kind."

My mentor then decided to look at the elder Lissesul, who presumably had more time for close encounters of the sexy kind. It took decades, but Valandil finally tracked down everyone who'd ever spent time in the royal palace. In the end, he did find something: Queen Orlinde, Galdor's wife, had once sent a chambermaid to the dungeons for stealing silverware."

"That sounds like something a queen would do, back in the good old days."

"Actually, such a small offense would warrant a flogging at most. And stealing silverware? That's something a scullery maid would do. How could a chambermaid manage it, when she's strictly an upstairs maid?"

"How am I to know what goes upstairs and downstairs? I'm just a country gentleman."

"A chambermaid takes care of bedrooms."

"Ah," I said, leaning back.

It seems Rosemary the Chambermaid had been very pretty and very young (only sixty-four.) What's more, she had the sort of body you didn't often see on elves—we're talking dangerous curves. She was an orphan rumoured to be part-halfling. She was certainly wild enough.

"She was willing, attractive, and had access to the king's bedchamber," Valandil said. "The fact that the queen sent her to the dungeons indicates that something happened."

"And what happened to her?" I asked, leaning forward.

"She was branded a thief and thrown out of the palace."

I grimaced. "Branded on the *face?*"

"The queen was certainly mad about something. A stigma like that would bar Rosemary from any decent work. My guess is she became a camp follower, and when the royal army passed through Corinthe she stayed there as a prostitute. This was fifteen hundred years ago."

"Sad story," I said. "When does my family enter the picture?"

"That's the interesting part. Your great-grandfather Dermethor brought home a baby at around the same time and acknowledged the infant as his son. His *only* son. I understand the wife wasn't pleased."

"Great-Grandma never warmed up to Grandpa Feanaro, but there wasn't much she could do since he was her husband's official heir. Hey, is that why he died at just nine hundred and twenty? Because he was a quarter halfling? And—hold it—does this make me part halfling?"

"Only one-sixteenth. It shouldn't be a problem when you take the throne."

"No wonder I hate elves," I said. It was a beat before I realized—

"Damn, you've convinced me!"

Valandil stroked his moustache and smiled. "The evidence is persuasive. As the last of your line—your parents being dead—you are automatically the crown prince."

"But what if I don't want to be king?"

"What you want doesn't matter! Finally, after almost a thousand wretched years, Brandish can once again be a kingdom. It doesn't even matter that you're descended from a half-breed whore—not if we mate you to a queen of the most exalted blood."

"After a few generations, nobody will be able to tell the difference, eh?"

"Exactly. The point is to maintain continuity!" Valandil now paced excitedly about. "It won't even be difficult to get you on the throne. I have powerful allies, and our position will be rock-solid when you fulfil the prophecy."

"Wait, the prophecy?"

Everyone knew that weird old poem. It had supposedly come to the best seers of the age, who had all written it down in exactly the same way.

"You do mix with the other races, don't you?" Valandil asked.

"I consider myself fairly cosmopolitan," I said. "But I don't have a silver hand, and I certainly don't know any dragons."

"Not yet, anyway."

I should've run screaming, because it's never a good sign when somebody starts waving around prophecies. The best you can hope for is that it's some kind of swindle, which means you're only going to lose your shirt. The worst you can hope for (because you're some kind of masochist) is that it's some kind of cult, which means you're about to become their virgin sacrifice.

Prophecies are never simple. They're always right, but you never understand them until they happen. Did you hear it properly? Is it in plain language, or is it in godawful verse? Can you try to prevent it, or will doing so actually fulfil the prophecy?

If the prophecy is about you, you're screwed. It sucks being The Chosen One. Your life isn't your own anymore.

"Any chance someone else fits the description? Maybe a long-lost sister or something?" I asked.

Valandil said nothing, only continued walking ahead of me. We were going deeper underground. I'd said something about dragons being extinct (nobody had seen one for a century) and he'd picked up the lantern and motioned me to follow.

I remembered what I'd said back in the alehouse, about the dragons having help dying out. "Master, are there no more dragons because of this prophecy?"

I thought quickly. It was possible that some of the same people who had supported the revolution had also reacted badly to the prophecy. They wouldn't be eager to see another king overturning their hard-earned status quo, so they'd... Wipe out an entire race to invalidate a prophecy?

Mind you, a dragon was a fifty-foot-long armoured death machine. It flew, it spewed fire, and it ate people. Not because it didn't know better (it could talk!) but because it *liked* how we tasted.

A single dragon would be a tough objective for an army, let alone a few self-appointed dragon hunters. The great scaly beasts were very hard to kill, all the books agreed on that. Yet the books also agreed that they had somehow disappeared over the last few centuries. From a stable population of several thousand, down to a handful, and down to nothing.

Suddenly I knew what it felt like to have true enemies.

"Master, are you trying to get me killed?" I said, and then stumbled on a rock.

"Get up, boy," Valandil said. He crouched and hauled me to my feet. Frail as he looked, my boots nearly left the floor—I remembered how strong earth mages could be.

"Don't you understand?" he said. "I am trying to restore this kingdom as well as your birthright. Brandish needs a king, whether or not you like it."

He put me down and picked up the lantern. "Anyway, if I'm right about this you'll have the best bodyguard in the world."

We continued down the tunnel. Dammit, how do I get myself into these situations? The passage widened into another chamber. It was a huge space, but the thing it contained was nearly as large. The massive shape crouched in the darkness until my master raised his lantern.

"Behold," he said, and I beheld a dragon.

Chapter 4

Findecano Elanesse, Lord Governor of Drystone, could do nothing as the soldiers attacked his daughter.

There were four of them. Each was fully-armoured and carried his weapon of choice. There was a sabre, a longsword, and two spears. Against this Meerwen fought barehanded, and all the boiled leather couldn't hide the fact that she looked small and frail.

Findecano gritted his teeth—the urge to throw a fireball was overpowering.

Being soldiers, they tried to surround her, but she kept backing away. They tried to move with her, but then she kicked the nearest man in the leg and he fell.

She jumped over him, punched him in the head, and jumped away. The other spearman went in, short jabs going for her head and neck, but she dodged and ducked until she got a hand on the spear. Then she swung her other arm and snapped the spear.

"Ha!"

The two swordsmen were old friends: the longsworder went high and the saberman went low. She stood and let them rain blows on her arms and shoulders, trusting in her leathers and her spell-hardened skin. Steel flashed and rang, but she held her ground.

She saw an opening—she darted forward and laid a fist on the saberman's cheek, then an uppercut to his midsection and chin. He fell with a dent in his breastplate.

The longsworder slashed at her face, forcing her to retreat. The second spearman joined him with their comrade's spear and they cut and sliced the air. Meerwen kicked at the longsworder and grabbed the spear in one hand. She pulled the spear, burying the head in the dirt, then caught the spearman and threw him at the longsword. The first spearman came up from behind and wrapped her in a bear hug. "We've got her now!"

The other two rushed her, and only a flurry of kicks kept them back. Meerwen jerked her head back, smashing into the grappler's face. She stomped on his toes, sank down, elbowed him in the gut, and threw him to the ground. Then she spun and kicked him in the ribs.

She snarled, and when the two swordsmen came at her she grabbed the longsword and started punching the wielder, punching and punching until he fell. A kick to the head and he was out.

It was just her and the saberman now, and they both pulled out the flashy stuff. For long seconds it was punch and counter punch, slash and spinning slash. The saberman danced and whirled his sword arm in deadly arcs. She kept her hands in contact with the steel, brushing the blade with her gloves. He cut low and she jumped, he cut low again and she lifted one foot and rammed it into his crotch. She stepped close, twisted the sabre from his hands, and head-butted him into unconsciousness.

The audience erupted into applause.

"Meerwen Elanesse wins!" said the Master of Ceremonies. "She has proven her mettle in honest battle!"

The leaders of the royal guard looked uneasy—women in the army were almost unheard of. So Findecano clapped and said, "My generals, is she not worthy of a commission?"

Under his gaze they could only nod.

Unaware of this, Meerwen beamed and bowed to the crowd as the medics rushed onto the field. Her leather armour was cracked, but she waved them aside.

"Well done, my daughter," Findecano said. "I see your time in the convent has been usefully spent."

"I'm glad to hear that, my father," Meerwen said as she walked up to the VIP stand. "Especially since you were against it in the first place."

"Those were some of the best fighters in the army. They were sons of soldiers, and grandsons of soldiers. I would not have thought it possible for a single person to defeat them, let alone barehanded and using human techniques."

"The humans have much to teach us, father. As do the other races."

"Everything they know, they learned from us. What can such people invent when their lives are so undisciplined?"

"The Fighting Nuns have plenty of discipline."

"For members of that oversexed race to take vows of chastity—let's just say they don't represent all of humanity. "

"But—"

"Enough. If we are to argue, let it be in private. Take my hand, my dear."

She took it, and they teleported home.

It was obvious to anyone that the Elanesse house was one of the oldest and finest mansions in the city. You only had to look at its seamless marble floors, its gold-inlaid walls, and, above all, its expansive floor plan. The servants always teleported to get from the kitchens to the dining hall, otherwise the food would get cold. Like many of the houses in the Palace Quarter it was built to the same plan as the king's residence, only slightly smaller.

There were other mansions as fine, but none as simply decorated as the Elanesse house. Findecano was not one for fine paintings, century-old tapestries, or eggshell-thin vases, though he could certainly afford them. Every stick of furniture was stark and useful—there wasn't a single conversation piece in the house.

You got the impression that he was an indifferent homeowner, until you realized that a complete lack of something was a statement on its own.

"I hope tonight's wine will be acceptable," Meerwen said, walking toward the house. "Elrond assured me it was one of his best vintages."

"I'm sure it is," he said. He caught up and took her arm. "Before we go in, would you walk with me?"

Meerwen frowned. "Is something wrong?"

"I merely wish for us to talk before I once again put on my public face. You know how these dinners are."

"I never understood why you'd have dinner guests who'd be happy to cut your throat."

"Politics, my dear. It makes for strange dining companions."

He was a grizzled old elf, well past the point where an elder could still pass for his junior. His face was lined and wrinkled, and age had filled out his frame. Yet there was strength in his limbs and quickness in his wits. He remained in his prime.

"I have missed these gardens," Meerwen said. "I see that Mother is still into orchids."

"She is," he said. The house was famous for its gardens. "Her main ambition is to cultivate a new variety." He looked at her. "Her other main ambition, that is, after ensuring her daughter's future."

Meerwen rolled her eyes. "Not this again, Daddy."

He grinned. "I can't stop being your father, can I? You know I've always wanted you to be happy."

"Am I not fulfilling my dreams? Granted, they're not what a young woman usually aspires to, but give me credit for originality."

They walked down a path that took them past flowerbeds and ornamental fountains. The land rose and fell, and at every turn the path revealed new things. This time three statues depicted the moment just after King Galdor's execution. There was the swordsman, his curved sword stuck in the chopping block. There was a younger Valandil, arms raised in anguish. Finally, there was the king, who in a bit of artistic license was standing and holding up his own head. It didn't seem to bother King Galdor that he was one black horse away from becoming a stereotype.

"These statues always used to scare me," Meerwen said. "I played everywhere but here."

"I remember. It didn't help that the cook used to tell you the statue of the king *was* the king, just petrified."

"And that he would come back to life if little girls didn't eat their vegetables."

They laughed. "I miss that time," Findecano said. "It seems only yesterday that you were a little girl who only wanted to read adventure stories and sneak off to the Halfling Theatre."

"I still read novels. Not much has changed."

"Yes. You are still completely uninterested in marriage."

"Daddy! I will marry when I'm ready. And when the right man presents himself."

"They're not exactly lining up, are they? Especially not after today's trial of arms."

She shrugged. "I'm advancing gender equality."

"Yes, but what about your family? You are my only child, and it's up to you to continue our House. To maintain continuity."

"I never liked the men you brought home."

"Why not? Nice boys, every one. What's more, they had coats of arms that went back generations, and not just to their grandfather's ennoblement. Do you know how many favours I burned just to give you a shot at a royal guard commission?"

"Am I hearing this from the elected Lord Governor? Is Drystone's champion of the common elf telling me I should marry into the aristocracy?"

He coughed. "Kings are obsolete, it is true, but the Houses still hold power. It wouldn't hurt if our blood had a bit of blue. After a few generations, nobody will be able to tell the difference."

They walked on, past artful tableaus of rock and sand. "In any case, Father, you probably shouldn't worry about never having in-laws."

Findecano raised an eyebrow. "Indeed? You've met someone?"

"More like ran into someone." She told him about the meeting in Elrond's Commonwealth.

"So this Angrod is an apprentice who goes drinking when he should be running errands?"

"Come on, you know masters never run out of chores. Why, even at the convent we were always chopping wood and carrying water. When we weren't printing postcards."

"When *I* was an apprentice—and my own apprenticeship was especially long, since I studied under several masters—I never had time for frivolous things."

"Tell that to Mother, since that's when you met her."

"I met him when?" someone said. They turned to see Tari Elanesse gliding toward them.

"My dear wife," Findecano said, and bowed. "How are you this evening?"

"Hello, Mother," Meerwen said, and curtsied.

"No need for formality," said the lady of the house. She was slender even for an elf, and tall. She had golden skin and auburn hair but otherwise looked remarkably like her daughter. "What's this about frivolous things?"

"It's nothing, Mother," Meerwen said, looking away.

"Meerwen has been telling me about a boy. And unlike the others, this one might have a chance."

"Really? Who is this fine man and what House is he from?"

"His name is Angrod Veneanar and he's a smartass," Meerwen said.

"But a smartass with a coat of arms," Findecano said. "And his chances look good—when has our daughter even *noticed* a boy?"

"It's not like that!" Meerwen said, turning red.

"Well, maybe it should be," Tari said. "You aren't getting younger, you know. When can we meet him?"

"I'm only a hundred and two," Meerwen said. "Plenty of time. And it's not my place to pursue him. He knows my name and where to find me."

Findecano was about to comment on how his daughter was challenging gender roles in the military, but not in romance, but thought better of it. "As a graduating apprentice he'll probably show up at the Royal Ball."

Meerwen's eyes lit up when he mentioned the biggest social event in Drystone. Then she looked worried. "The Royal Ball? But I have nothing to wear!"

"Tomorrow your father will call in the best tailors in the city," Tari said. "In the meantime, why not get dressed for dinner? You have just enough time if you go now."

"I'll do that," Meerwen said. "Mother, Father. We will talk more later."

Husband and wife watched as their child hurried into the house. Findecano smiled. "Young love."

Tari looked to him with a frown. "This Angrod, isn't he apprenticed to Valandil the Royalist?"

"Yes," Findecano said. "By all reports Angrod is a nice boy, if a bit wild."

"You're still having his master followed?"

"Even when he teleports. He was never good at keeping secrets, or we wouldn't have heard about his little project."

They walked arm in arm down the meandering path, stopping to enjoy a topiary animal here and there.

"Is it likely, you think?" she asked.

"That he'll find a missing heir? I shouldn't think so. Still, there *is* a prophecy, so better safe than sorry."

They looked at a topiary dragon, which reared up like the real thing. You expected it to snarl and breathe fire any moment.

"I hope this doesn't call for some pruning," he said.

"Sometimes things need cutting," she said. "Otherwise they lose their shape."

"Is the shape so important?"

She looked at him. "Don't be ridiculous. We've spent centuries cultivating our garden, and I should hate to abandon it now. Sometimes the situation calls for the hedge trimmer and sometimes it calls for the scythe."

"I would hate to lose the city's best builder."

"Would you rather the city lose its Lord? That would be a true loss to the city. We are so close to accomplishing our goal. Our supporters rule Pithe, Vergath, Mithish, and Lamemheth. Only Corinthe in the north remains adamant."

"I will not crown myself king," he said, but he was stroking his chin.

"What's a crown got to do with it? We shall merely create room for a prime minister. The best man will inevitably fill that space." She looked at him and smiled. "My husband, *you* will inevitably fill that space."

Chapter 5

"S*hiiiiiit!*"

I jumped away from the dragon and fell on my arse. I scurried back, my mind reaching for every bit of defensive magic I knew. Flame wall? I'd burn all the oxygen! Ice wall? Not enough moisture!

The floor rose up in front of me, coming to hundreds of sharp points. A palisade of stone rose up, every jagged edge pointed at the dragon. Razor-sharp stalactites jutted from the ceiling, ready to impale the huge reptile if it so much as blinked.

...

It didn't. What I thought was a living, breathing dragon was in fact a gigantic statue.

"Oh, very funny, Valandil. Ha ha. Oh, ha ha ha. Is this my graduation prank? You really went through a lot of effort. That statue looks so lifelike."

"Look again, my apprentice," Valandil said, his face serious. "Use your other senses."

"What, did someone paint *Angrod is a wanker* in ultraviolet paint?"

"Use. Your. Other. Senses."

I shrugged and opened my Sight.

—and backpedalled further, for I'd glimpsed a living aura inside the stone. "Holy hell, the dragon's alive!"

The Sight is not like hearing or smell. No sense organ gives us this ability, although it relies on all of them. The Sight is nothing less than applied synaesthesia, using one's existing senses to make sense of information gained through magic.

If you've ever heard a song that made you see fireworks, or eaten something that tasted like music, you know what I mean. Elves can turn it on or off and some scholars say we evolved it to deal with the monotony of a long lifespan. A person can only have so many new experiences, but the Sight can extend the novelty for a long while. It's an excellent way to get new perspectives.

I'd *Seen* a stone dragon wrapped in electricity. It crackled and flowed throughout the monstrous body, drawing patterns on its skin and shining brightly through its bones. It was alive, and yet it was entirely stone.

"A petrified dragon," I said. "Amazing!"

"The prophecy calls for at least one dragon, and as far as I know this is the last one alive."

"I wouldn't call it alive," I said. "It's basically frozen. Who did this?"

"A powerful elven mage did it in the fifth century as a favour to the dragon. Take a look at its back."

I walked around—and grimaced. It was a grisly sight, even though everything was bone-dry and marble-white. Gigantic claws had torn long wounds into the dragon's flesh and huge jaws had bitten out great chunks. The bone showed in many places and the spine was nearly severed.

"Wyverns," Valandil said, and I winced. They were related to dragons, but smaller. They couldn't talk and lacked the forelimbs of dragons, but they made up for it through sheer viciousness. This dragon had apparently run into a flight of them.

"The mage wasn't skilled enough to heal it, so instead he turned the dragon to stone, preserving it against the day of its resurrection."

"I'm assuming you've tried waking it up."

"Of course I have. I've been trying for years! Transmutation at that level is a lost art, however. For all my experience, I could do nothing. Then again, maybe I'm not the man destiny has chosen."

I crossed my arms. "I have to tell you, Master, I don't feel particularly chosen. You don't really think I can bring him back, do you?"

"Indulge me," Valandil said, placing his hand on my shoulder. "Just make a serious attempt, and I will release you from all of your obligations as an apprentice."

"All right, old man," I said. "But only because you bribed me."

I walked around to the dragon's head and looked into its calcified eyes. Then I began the Working.

I remember the first time I saw Valandil build.

It was early on the construction site. It was cold, too, so I wore a coat. A crowd was waiting to see the master at work.

Valandil paced the site, inspecting the raw materials piled around the lot. The little family that had hired us was right beside me. The wife was smiling, the husband was beaming, and the little girl was hopping up and down. Everyone sipped hot chocolate and waited for the action.

Valandil shrugged off his robe and tossed it at me. I caught it and he walked to the middle of the lot. His skin was gray and somewhat loose, but the muscles beneath spoke of wiry power. He reached the centre of the site and planted his feet in the earth.

The mounds of gravel, sand, and dirt turned into fountains. They simply fell upward and the builder-mage vanished in the dust cloud. In less than a second he'd dug the foundations with magic, and now everything was drifting down. I couldn't see it, but I knew that sand, slag, and gravel were mixing to form concrete. Water leaped out of the nearby ditch, overflowed its banks, and capering across the grass.

Valandil held the entire design in his head: Everything found itself falling into place. There were sparks as iron ore turned to steel in mid-air, then twisted into wire. The walls grew, layer-by-layer—thin, light, and extremely strong. We could see Valandil moving as though underwater, pushing and pulling at the swirling clouds. He was like a potter, only he worked with his entire body as he turned in place and shaped the house around him.

Sand became ropes of glass and became part of the walls. The walls steamed as the heat was pulled from them. The famous white sand returned to the earth as flakes of ultra-hard glass. The flakes blew against the walls and melded into a beautiful gloss.

Still Valandil worked. He danced around the building, adding details there and there. The muscles on his back strained against themselves. Sweat ran freely. It took fifteen minutes more, but he finished the house to thunderous applause.

It was a Working of a master, but it was nothing compared to the transmutation of living flesh. Shapeshifters just reconfigure their tissues, and even the best doctors can only accelerate the body's natural healing process. Turning flesh to stone (and vice versa) was the highest of high magic. It gave you the means to conquer death, to become something like a god.

And Valandil, who always said my spells were sloppy, actually thought I could do that?

I stared into the dragon's amber eyes and willed it to life.

...

I focused my mind upon the dragon's form, calling up the powers that resided in the space around me. I tensed, adding my own strength. The air thickened with magical potential.

...

I was sweating. My face was red. Sweat ran down my forehead and my irises grew and shank independently of each other. I thought I caught movement in a corner. Still nothing.

...

"Keep going," Valandil said.

I took another tack. I focused my Sight upon the rocky horror. Incredibly, the long-dead mage had preserved the dragon's cell structure even as he mineralized the flesh. It looked like I had a chance to revive this gigantic lawn ornament. I concentrated on the structure and my mind opened like a flower.

There were trillions of cells in the dragon's body, and for a long moment of agony I could see them all at once, everything working and humming and ALIVE. I saw everything. *Everything.* For a time I forgot myself, so intense was my need to dream a dragon into the waking world. I saw a fossilized heart pump crystallized blood through arteries of glass. I saw brittle bones move and fragile muscles flex—I saw myself clenching my hands and crying. The ground steamed around my knees. The air grew hot and my tears boiled away. I saw the heart, that red beating fist, as it pumped fire through arteries of sand. I saw… I saw…

I think I screamed. For sure I fell back, clawing at my eyes, trying to get at the afterimages of tens of trillions of animal cells. I screamed and toppled, and just before I blacked out the dragon reared its head and shattered its neck. The head fell free, smashing into the ground in a thousand pieces.

"Angrod? Can you hear me, boy?"

I opened my eyes. Valandil loomed over with the lantern, looking concerned.

"How long was I out?"

"Not long. I just elevated your legs."

"My throat is sore. What are my legs resting on?"

"A piece of dragon."

I tried to sit up—and instantly regretted it. I lay back, suddenly dizzy, and automatically drew strength from the ground.

The background magic exists all around us, but it's helpful to frame it in terms of the four elements. If you're working earth magic, you draw power from the earth, and so on.

I lay there, eyes closed, as my mind reasserted itself and the nausea fell away. I got to my feet without help. My feet had indeed been resting on a bit of dragon. The head and much of the neck were scattered all over the floor. I opened my Sight and looked at the rest of the body.

"It's dead," I said. "No more aura. So much for prophecies."

The old man looked like he might cry. I'd have patted him on the shoulder, but we weren't that close. He shook his head. "Centuries in stasis, only to end up like this."

"I tried, Master. Can't say I didn't make an effort. Hey, maybe this was what they meant by a dragon bowing to me? You must admit, its head can't get any lower to the ground."

"Did you see how it moved at the end? Almost like it was coming to its feet... how do you feel?"

"Like my brain grew two sizes. It's worse than a Monday hangover."

"We should be going. I'm going to need my supporters more than ever. To build your case. We'll need to establish a clear line of succession, one way or another."

"Oh, joy."

We left that dark and lonely cavern, now a tomb.

Master and apprentice were long gone when the spy made his move.

He walked in absolute dark, trusting in his Sight to keep him clear of the debris. This far underground the temperature gradients weren't enough for him to see by infrared, so he relied on echolocation. Clicking his tongue, he found the tunnel entrance and started for the surface.

Now the cavern was a tomb.

Findecano Elanesse opened the door to his study. It was night, and dinner was long since over.

It had gone smoothly, as his wife's dinner parties tended to do. Connections had been made, alliances maintained, and truces reaffirmed. The food had been good, too. Afterward he had spent a couple of hours discussing things with his wife. They chatted until it was time for his private meditation.

The study was in the tallest tower of the house. He stared out of the western window, which overlooked the sea and gave him a view of the moonlight on the waves. It was a colourless sort of light and he much preferred the glow of a bustling Drystone. The lighthouse, further up the coast, was a beacon in many ways.

He took in the view for a moment, then turned to his personal library. He took a book from the shelf and ran a hand over the buttery leather. He opened, the book, stroked his beard—and hurled a bolt of power. It smashed into empty air and suddenly the spy was on the floor, half-frozen and chattering.

"H-hold it, milord, hold it! Ch-chill out!"

Findecano glowered at him. "Dragon-slayer. Mage-killer. King's assassin. What do you think you're doing, standing veiled in my private chambers?"

The spy got to his feet, brushing ice from his cloak. "I was only keeping operational secrecy. Wasn't sure you'd be alone."

"You may be my agent, but I haven't forgotten who trained you. The Elendil Order does not play well with others."

"I said I was sorry, milord."

"No, you didn't. Never mind. Report."

The spy recounted what he had seen in the cave by the sea. Findecano poured them cups of wine and heated them in his hands. The two elves sat across from each other, in front of the fireplace and sipped from the steaming cups.

"So you're saying the old crackpot finally found his prince?"

"And it's his own apprentice too," the spy said. "It seems Valandil suspected a royal connection even before he accepted Angrod."

"And now the lad knows? This is unfortunate."

The spy shrugged. "So we kill him and the old man too. No worries—I can make it look like all sorts of accidents. The good news is that dragons are officially extinct. That was almost certainly the last one alive, and now it's gravel. With your permission I will tell this to the head of my order."

Findecano nodded. "It's good to be rid of those terrible reptiles."

"What about the old fool and the young fool? When shall we be rid of them?"

"I will think on this," Findecano said, and sipped his wine. "The timing must be right. You may go now."

"Yes, milord." The spy finished his drink and got up to leave, but stopped. "I was wondering how you saw through my veil. I could've sworn it was perfect."

The wizard laughed. "It nearly was. You bent the light around you, synchronized your breathing to mine, and even smoothed the air currents—but you couldn't stop your feet from pressing on the floor. I could feel your weight as if we were walking on a drum. You would have done better to stand next to something heavy, like the bookshelf."

"And then you wouldn't have sensed me?"

"No, but it still would've been the smart thing to do. I advise you to practice the rest of the week, because I'll need you to shadow Valandil at the Governor's Ball.

"Will do, milord. I'll be going now."

As Valandil watched, the spy exuded droplets from his pores. The pure water gathered on his skin and clothes, which remained dry. The water became a film, a bubble covering his entire body. It became a mirror. It turned transparent. The camouflage was complete.

Valandil nodded in approval. As long as they both stood still, the spy was invisible. The distortion in the air bowed and the spy teleported away.

The Lord Governor of Drystone shook his head and turned back to his book, *How to Make Friends and Outlive Your Enemies*.

Chapter 6

I woke up and groaned. It was as if an entire dwarven mining crew was digging for treasure in my skull. I could've saved them the trouble—there wasn't anything valuable in there.

I'd just managed to swing out of bed and start washing off the eye gunk when the water basin turned into a goddamn face.

"Waaaugh!" I said, and fell on my arse.

The sending was the head and shoulders of a beautiful blonde elf girl. It looked around, unseeing, and began to speak. "Angrod Veneanar? The Lord Governor would like to see you later. It's regarding your audience."

"My what? The Lord Governor? What have I done?"

It was Findecano Elanesse, no question. Only his office could get past the wards in every house. His people couldn't spy on us, but they *could* scare the morning piss out of me. The secretary continued:

"Remember, all graduating apprentices are required to undergo an exit interview at the Mage's Citadel. Lord Governor Elanesse has graciously accepted the responsibility. He will await you at your earliest convenience. Say eight of the clock?"

"I'll be there."

She looked down. I'm sure she was just guessing, but for a second I thought she could see me. She smiled. "Thank you for your time."

The shaping of water splashed back into the basin.

"Bloody hell," I said. "I'm not going to wash my face in that."

The Mage's Citadel is in the Merchant Quarter, not because mages cater to merchants, but because that's where the best restaurants are. It used to have its own district far from the rest of the city, but then the elder wizards got tired of the commute and relocated their headquarters. And when I say relocated, I mean the massive fortress had been teleported in one piece.

It loomed over the shops and temples, a gleaming tower of arcane lore. Most buildings only had a thin superceramic coating, but the Citadel was plated in the stuff. Its walls laughed at catapults.

Then again, considering how it was packed full of combat magicians, each worth a battery of siege engines, the armoured architecture seemed rather overkill. What force would be foolish enough to attack it?

I made my way down the cobblestoned streets—the citadel was warded against teleportation. Also, you don't want to appear suddenly in a roomful of combat mages. I could already see them as I drew closer to the building. They swaggered in their gray and black robes, the air crackling with the spell-glyphs they held at the forefront of their minds. They looked at my white apprentice's robes and sneered. Gods, but I hated them.

All magic users know a few defensive tricks, but combat mages specialize in offense. They cultivate hair-trigger tempers, the better to channel destructive energies. They favour either fire magic, for obvious reasons, or air magic, so they can hover around shooting lightning.

Every Great House has a few on the payroll because they offer the best firepower for weight. At the same time, the job doesn't attract the sanest types, and it certainly does nothing for their emotional stability. They often fight among themselves while everyone else runs for cover. Two combat mages will face each other across the street and stare each other down. The first one to blink gets a fireball in the eyes.

They like to do this at noon, but this doesn't discourage the lunch crowd at all. Say what you will about Drystone, but their gourmets are hardcore.

Now and again I saw a red robe. The black and gray robes avoided them, and with good reason—you don't get reach the third and highest rank of combat mage without spilling lots of blood. Each red mage was a master of at least two schools of magic, either of which could turn a stronghold into a crater.

The most unnerving thing about them is their utter calm. They've bluffed down entire armies with nothing but a steely gaze.

The Citadel stood apart from the other buildings, in the centre of its own park. There were decorative trees here and there, but I knew they would be razed to the ground as soon as there was trouble. The Citadel may be a school, but first it was a fortress.

The guards let me in and I found my way up to one of the lecture halls. I was fifteen minutes early but the Lord Governor was already waiting.

Findecano Elanesse wore red robes trimmed in gold. Oh, shit.

"You must be Angrod. I've heard good things about you from the various professors. And from your mentor, of course."

"They are too kind," I said, and bowed.

Findecano smiled and returned the bow. It looked like he was genuinely pleased to see me. Like Valandil he was old enough that even a human could tell he was no longer young. Also like Valandil, Findecano was one of the few elves who could grow a beard worth a damn. I liked him instantly.

"You *were* expecting an interview, weren't you?" he asked. In addition to his red mage's robes (holy hell!) he wore a red peaked cap and sported blue tattoos on his cheeks.

"Of course," I said. "Although I wasn't expecting… well, you, sir."

He laughed. "I don't often do this, but as a senior mage I am well enough qualified. I was going over a list of incoming guild members and your name sounded familiar. I hear you've met my daughter."

"It was an accident, sir."

"You wouldn't have gone out of your way to speak to her?"

"That is, uh, a happy accident."

Findecano laughed again. "I'm joking. Old Telerunya doesn't take on many apprentices—he wouldn't have me, back in the day—so it's noteworthy when he does. Do you see yourself as a builder like him?"

I thought about it. "It's challenging work, and worthwhile… but my heart's not in it."

Findecano nodded. "Walk with me."

We left the lecture hall and climbed to the battlements. The Citadel had a commanding view of Drystone, naturally enough. Build partially on the sea, the city had an octagonal plan. We were in the Merchant Quarter, with its schools and stores, but I could see the other districts as well. There was the Manufacturing Quarter, where artisans had their shops, and there was the Old Quarter, where everyone else lived. Directly opposite the Merchant Quarter was the Palace Quarter, full of mansions and parks.

All the districts were connected by wide thoroughfares, which were canals in some places and roads in others.

"Like what you see?" asked the Lord Governor. "It's a devil to run, but it does look good from a distance."

I had to agree. Under the early morning sun even the Old Quarter was clean and bright.

"Do you know why apprentices are interviewed before they are released from their masters?" Findecano asked. "And why the interviewer is always a combat mage of at least the Second rank?"

I thought about it. "Apprentices are tested four times, by four different masters, to confirm that they are ready to become journeymen." I thought some more. "There is one final test to determine whether they are worthy of guild membership, but nobody told me what it was about. Will you test my battle magic? I'm afraid I haven't prepared any spells."

He shook his head. "It's more of a morals test than a magic test. The exit interview is to find out whether you're the sort of person who should be walking around with a wizardly education. Of course, we try to catch the bad ones before the training starts, but you'd be surprised how many would-be evil overlords manage to reach journeyman level."

"What happens to them?" I asked, already knowing the answer.

Findecano grinned. "The interviewer... takes care of them."

Eep.

"But no pressure," he continued. "So, have you read the Necronomicon, or are you familiar with it?"

"What?"

He laughed and slapped my shoulder. "Just kidding, boy! I'm still joking."

I sagged in relief.

"But if you turn out bad I'll kill you."

When I'd calmed down enough, we actually had a pleasant chat about magical theory. I'd written a paper on it, and Valandil had read it.

"So you don't believe we're native to this world?" he asked.

"No, sir. The natural philosophers and taxonomists keep digging up evidence."

There were fossils. Strange fossils. The remains of animals that no longer existed, so different from anything today we can only call them alien. They didn't just lack modern-day descendants—they were completely unrelated to anything alive.

"It's like a desert island. Plants wash up on shore and birds deposit seeds in their droppings. Animals arrive by flying, swimming, or clinging onto driftwood. The island develops a complete ecosystem, which in time becomes highly specialized. And then the volcano erupts, wipes the slate clean, and the process starts over."

Findecano scratched his beard. "It makes sense. There are things in the deepest oceans with too many arms and eyes. An elven destroyer once managed to catch one, but it was so foul the sailors couldn't even sell it for dog food."

"That's right, sir. And the dragons must have been survivors from an earlier wave, because apart from wyverns they had no relatives."

"Should we be worried about a volcano?"

"I think we should worry more about invasive species. A monk once experimented with peas. When raised in an amplified magic field, each successive generation grew more magical. They started extracting water from the air, making their own fertilizer, and walking."

"I remember those. They'd follow you around until you gave them a drink. But they didn't last long—something about low pollen counts."

"The pea plants grew longer-lived," I said. "And also less fertile. Does that sound familiar?"

"Are you saying elves are turning into pea-plants?"

"Er, more like turning into dragons. Awesomely powerful, tremendously long-lived, but increasingly rare. It's one reason we haven't been as active in the world."

"What the hell was a monk doing with pea plants?"

"I understand that between poverty and chastity there wasn't much else to do."

"What about the dwarves, the humans, and all the other humanoid species? How is it they can, er, interbreed with elves?"

"Different waves, sir. We share a common ancestor, but presumably we arrived first and the others followed later."

Findecano shivered. "I'd prefer the volcano."

Chapter 7

I cut low, following through with my other stick, but Meerwen leaped clear and swung a kick at my head. I bobbed, then stepped away as she kicked at my face. Damn she was fast. She took the offensive and started jabbing and I had to bring up the sticks to keep her away.

I'd gotten through the interview well enough—I was still alive, which meant I'd passed, according to Findecano. He saluted me, then teleported away (in the warded Citadel!) so I collected the shreds of my dignity and left. Valandil didn't need me for the rest of the day. He had released me from my duties, in any case, so I decided to head to the nearest training hall. Beating on a practice dummy seemed a good way to spend the rest of the morning.

I had just stepped onto the mat when Meerwen appeared. Like me, she wore a sleeveless shirt, loose shorts, and light shoes, elves preferring to train in as little armour as possible. She had wrapped her hands and forearms in bandages. I asked about them.

"I'm not hurt," she said. "This is just what I wear when sparring."

"So you really fight without weapons?" I said. "Isn't that handicapping yourself?"

"The body is a more versatile weapon than any implement."

"Right," I said.

"Why don't I show you? No magic enhancement, of course."

"I just met your father, and I doubt he'd be happy if I beat you up."

She laughed. "I promise you that won't happen. Now grab your little sticks."

I reached behind me and pulled the sticks from hammerspace. "I should warn you, these aren't for sparring. They're solid ironwood."

"Get into the ring, pussy."

We stepped into the ring.

Elves train to fight from a young age. We shy from high-risk activities, but we make an exception with the martial arts. Although accidents happen, it's more dangerous not to learn. After all, if you don't know how to handle yourself in a fight, someone will always be too happy to force you into one.

Our fighting arts are entirely weapon-based. What's the point of barehanded fighting when at least one person will be armed in real combat? If you're the unlucky one, your goal should be to disarm the other guy, then punish him for being so stupid.

I knew plenty of ways to take away someone's weapon, but the fact that Meerwen didn't have one was confusing. Still, I live to improvise. I stepped forward and swung, my off hand ready for an overhead cut. The plan was to use my superior reach to batter her from a distance.

She responded by parrying my first blow, then chopping at my main hand.

"Ow!" I said, almost dropping the stick. I followed up with the other one, but she leaned away and planted a punch on my cheek.

"Hah!"

I cut low, trying to sweep her legs out, but she jumped and hooked a kick to my face. I dodged that, but she kept at me with the punches, just going bam-bam-bam, and I had to whirl my sticks to keep her away.

"I'm surprised you're still using training weapons," Meerwen said.

"Hey, I like these sticks."

Elves train in the Nine Weapons. The training hall was full of examples and my peripheral vision noted at least one of each. There was a blue-skinned elf practicing with double sticks. His opponent wielded a wooden sword and knife. To their right was a burly elf doing solo drills with a waster and shield. That took care of the paired weapons.

A brother and sister—both blonde—sparred with spear and staff. The boy wielded the spear aggressively, while his sister took the defensive. It looked like they'd practiced for decades. Across the practice space an older elf hacked at a t-shaped post with a longsword. So went the two-handed weapons.

A whirling three-way fight had developed between a sabre, a rapier, and a knife: the one-handed weapons.

Meerwen batted my sticks aside, then came in with elbows. One caught me in the chest and I stumbled. Damn, the Elanesses were giving me a hard time. She took a running leap and buried me under punches and kicks. She followed hard rights with harder elbows—palm strikes with backhands. She tore the sticks from my hands and threw them into hammerspace.

"Now *I* have the advantage," she said.

I covered up, but her hardened limbs found openings. I blocked low and she struck high. I blocked high—she shattered my guard with an axe kick. I kicked and she hit my leg with a bone-cracking hammerfist. Then she grabbed the back of my neck and butted me in the head.

The hall had gone silent. Nobody had seen fighting like this. Most of us knew a little boxing and grappling, but this was something else entirely.

I charged, but she just picked me up and slammed me onto the mat.

Need a little help? someone asked. What?

If you want to win this fight (and reclaim some self-respect) follow my lead.

Who are you?

Enough talk!

I felt myself rise to my feet. Not get up, or stand up, but *rise up*. I was hauled to my feet as though by invisible hands. My arms lifted as if on strings and my hands became claws.

Meerwen raised an eyebrow. "Never seen that before."

I turned one hand and beckoned her closer. "Come on if you think you're hard enough."

She darted forward, but my arms lashed out like snakes, catching, blocking, striking. My feet flashed under me, the stance wide but fluid. I danced around her, my hands a blur. A flurry of claws to the face to disorient her, then a double body blow with palm-heel strikes. My hands wove in and out, finding the smallest of openings and hitting with hardened fingers. In the distance I heard kettledrums.

She kicked and clubbed me with her forearms, but my hands were there to hook and catch. I pushed her away with a front kick and she froze in a fighting stance.

"What's happened to you?" she asked. "You're radiating power—you're cheating!"

"I'm not!"

I leaped, covering most of the circle, and Meerwen got her hands in front of her, took a deep breath, and went "HDAAH!" The sound hit me like a blow and I staggered.

"Wind magic?" I said.

She grinned. "Well, you started it."

She came in hard, the magic adding speed to her punches. Time slowed. My hands went out lazily to intercept, to deflect. To trap and to catch. I saw my hand whip around and slap her on the cheek."

"Ooh, that is *it!*" she said. She pounded the floor and rose up, the ground shuddering as she gathered power from it. Her skin took on a shell-like quality as the earth magic reinforced her skin. She brought her hands up and her knuckles cracked as she made them into fists.

Crap.

I ran out of the hall and Meerwen flew after. We headed for the thicket of poles where elves trained in forest combat. I got there first and turned to face her. I dodged and her fist brushed past, smashing into one of the heavy posts.

"Ugh," she said.

I smiled and wove among the poles. I ducked her side kick and retreated deeper into cover. It was like a bamboo forest. It was easy to slip or block her attacks. My hands darted this way and that, catching her around the eyes and face.

"Ow!"

A nearby post exploded into splinters. She'd grabbed it and crushed it with her bare hand. She raged, not holding back anymore. Her flailing arms smashed left and right, shattering the poles and bringing them down around us.

Still I fought. Time slowed again. I slapped aside a falling tree trunk, sidestepped another. I got both eyes on Meerwen and waggled my head in a circle, triangulating. I waited for her to jerk her head just so, and then my head shot forward and vomited fire.

As in literally vomited. Everything I'd had for breakfast (soss and egg!) came back up, changing all the way. Part of me was running a transmutation spell, turning the half-digested contents into *napalm*. I spat sticky fire at Meerwen's face.

Her eyes grew wide. She got her hands up, took a breath, and yelled "HDAAH!" The blast hurled burning droplets in all directions. I dove behind a tree as the whole thicket turned into a forest fire.

The training hall's supervising mage ran out, saw the inferno, and teleported a ton of seawater over our heads. It splattered like a gigantic egg, ending our sparring session.

Meerwen stared at me, her short hair plastered all over her face. "What the holy blazing *fuck* was that?"

I picked myself up. The entire mock forest was a charred mess, with many of the posts broken and fallen. There was something—I put a hand down my pants. Her eyes grew wider.

"Sorry," I said, taking out a confused fish. Absently I put it into my pocket. "I don't know what came over me."

"Where'd you learn to fight like that?"

I shrugged. "Here and there." Actually, I didn't have a clue. "I'm just full of surprises."

"How are you two idiots going to pay for this?" demanded the combat mage. I sighed. I was getting a headache again.

"I heard you demolished a training hall," Valandil said, "and that your opponent was the daughter of Elanesse."

"It started out as a friendly match, believe it or not."

We were having dinner at Biggo's Bar and Grill. You know the place: wood panelling, comfortable wicker chairs, and home cooking, if you shared your home with barbecue-loving bachelors.

"They say you fought her unarmed, and in a most unusual way."

"I don't know how. It's like I suddenly remembered how to fight without weapons."

"Those of royal blood can call upon the skills and the wisdom of their ancestors. Could this be another bit of evidence? Interesting, that this happened when you fought a member of that upstart House."

I rolled my eyes. "She gave as much as she got. Like she said, there are advantages to being the daughter of one of the greatest mages alive—she learned spells with her bedtime stories."

Valandil sniffed. "I suppose it's commendable, that she should work hard to make up for her shortcomings."

"I don't know if she had any shortcomings—she took it all and just kept coming." I saw the waiter with our orders. "Why don't we just enjoy our meal?"

We fell to eating, and for a while nobody talked. The air was thick with savoury smells (even the salads were fattening) and a halfling band was playing thumping good music. Elves are supposed to be the best musicians, if you like day-long instrumental solos, but nothing beat halfling music for immediacy. The quartet was inspiring more than a little foot-tapping.

"I wish they wouldn't play such noise," Valandil said, finishing his plate.

"It brings in the young crowd."

He frowned. "Since when did our society become obsessed with youth? I expect you will change that once you take the throne. I have news, by the way."

I was having a sip of wine, so I gestured for him to continue.

"I've just heard from our allies—they're willing to support us once we go public with your lineage. And I've just devised a family tree that avoids any recent scandal."

"How'd you manage that?"

"Did you know, even without the maid Rosemary you were high in the line of succession? If we suppose a few of your great-great-grandfathers were born on the wrong side of the blanket, your name rises to the top."

I stared at him. "So by making bastards of my ancestors, you make me the biggest bastard of all?"

"Think of the glory," said Valandil. "I'll be announcing it at the Lord Mayor's Ball. Wouldn't that surprise Findecano?"

I groaned. I'd been getting on so well with Meerwen.

"Chin up, my dear apprentice. And I must thank you for the meal—that was an excellent fish."

"Caught it myself," I said.

In a curtained booth across the restaurant, the spy finished his rare steak and listened to the pair of fools. Although the place buzzed with music and conversation, it was simple for him to internalize his water magic. He was seeing in black-and-white, but his senses of taste and hearing were excellent.

The spy shook his head. They didn't know shit about running a conspiracy. He would report what he'd just learned and with any luck Findecano would give him permission to kill at least one of them.

He smiled and wiped his chin. He wished it would be the both of them, because then he could make it look like a lover's quarrel, and those were always good for diverting suspicion. Everyone would be too scandalized to question the evidence.

Chapter 8

The Royal Ball was okay, if you like extravagant luxury. All of the city's glitterati wore their finest and their flashiest. Loads of silk brocade and lace, miles of fur and velvet, and everything garnished with rubies and pearls. And that was just the men.

We were in the biggest hall in the royal palace. It glowed from the light of a hundred chandeliers. Each was gilt bronze (dwarves being expert goldsmiths) and boasted dozens of gas lamps. The light was warm and bright, the better to show off the costumes and the food.

Normally I consider Biggo's to be the height of cuisine, but jaded elven aristocrats demand so much more. Delicacies from all over the world, prepared with only the most expensive ingredients and served in ornate arrangements. There was roc pâté, slow-roasted wyvern, and wild halfling steak. The smell around the buffet tables was so rich and thick you could almost put it on your plate.

For dessert, there were one thousand choices, each an epicure's dream. There were marzipan swans, candied scorpions, and chocolates filled with brandy and venom. There were butterfly ices, civet cakes, and mango floats covered in gold foil. To keep everything from melting there were mages dressed as waiters— they stood behind the tables and extracted the heat from the dishes.

Tari Elanesse kept things casual. Apart from a few opening speeches, there wasn't much of a program. It was more of a giant cocktail party—everyone was free to circulate from the tables to the dance floor.

Valandil came striding up to me, more than a little drunk. "Angrod, my boy, it's good to see you. In less than an hour I shall make the announcement that will change history."

"Have you been hitting the rum balls?"

"You could be more enthusiastic, but it doesn't matter. Once you are king you can do *anything*. Within reason, of course. You can't neglect the kingdom and you'll have to produce a royal heir. An heir and a spare, if you can manage it."

I wrung my hands. "I don't see how this can work."

"Oh, but it will! Appoint me as your personal advisor and I will always be at your side. We will establish a dynasty to last ten thousand years!"

"Urgh," I said. I was getting a headache again. Valandil patted me on the back and wandered toward the champagne. I would have headed to the gardens, but then Meerwen was before me.

"Hello," she said. "You clean up nicely."

I bowed. "And you look stunning." She wore a light blue dress. Her short hair was embellished with a silver tiara.

She tilted her head. "Are you sure? It seems everyone has eyes for the capran ambassador. Who would have thought to combine a plunging back with an open-front skirt?"

"You must admit, Her Excellency has great legs. And who else has jewels set in her hooves and horns?"

"Randy little goat," Meerwen muttered. I was about to ask whether she meant the Ambassador or me, but then she smiled. "Would you care to dance?"

"Of course," I said. I offered my arm and led her to the dance floor.

Unlike the halfling music from earlier that week, the soundtrack of this ball was strictly elven, and highbrow at that. It used no instruments invented less than a thousand years ago and all the composers were generations dead. Given our life spans, that's a lot.

The dancers flowed in precise geometries, sometimes in circles and sometimes in stars. Partners broke away, sidestepped, and paired up with new partners. They orbited and spun, leaped together and apart, linked hands and made lines.

Mastering a single dance took decades, which was why only elves ventured onto the floor. The humans and the dwarves stood to the sidelines, looking on with admiration and envy.

"You've got moves, Meerwen," I said.

"Thanks. You dance well too."

My headache was definitely worsening. What started as a low-key buzzing had become a pounding, as if something were trying to get out. It must've showed on my face, because Meerwen frowned. "Is something wrong?" she asked. "Am I doing this okay?"

"It's not you," I said. "I don't feel well."

"Do you want to stop?"

I shook my head. "I can last through this dance. It sounds like it's almost done."

I saw Valandil heading toward the stage. He had a scroll under his arm, no doubt evidence for when he proclaimed me as the next king.

Stupid old man, to think he could bend a dragon to his will. I should've killed him in that cave.

What?

I was sweating in my formal outfit. My skin itched so hard it was almost crawling off my back. Coloured shadows swam behind my eyes. I was suddenly hungry, but when I glanced at the buffet it might as well have been a pile of rocks. I turned my attention to my dance partner. *She* looked tasty.

"Angrod? Are you okay?"

I swallowed, trying not to drool. Sweet, sweet flesh. I wanted to tear off her legs and eat them raw.

"Angrod?"

Distantly I noted that my master had climbed onto the stage. The music had stopped and he was already activating a voice-amplification spell. It was a simple enough bit of wind magic, but he still went for the old joke: "Is this thing on?"

I was shaking and cramping, but managed to hold together as the crowd turned to the stage.

"As you recall, I was advisor to the last king, Galdor Lissesul. He was a wise, fair sovereign who treated everyone with respect. Most people don't know he formed the council that currently governs Brandish. He created it with the express purpose of making sure that no single person was all-powerful. It is a testament to his foresight that our country has survived so long with an empty throne."

"But that will change."

He took a beat to glance around. Findecano and Tari Elanesse stood to one side, their faces unreadable. My master continued:

"As you know, His Highness was executed by a mob during a famine. It was a most shameful treatment of a great man, one who had spent his last days searching for a solution. I was there when they killed him, and I shall remember it as long as I live. I wept that day, I am not ashamed to say, and I wept again when I heard of Prince Errol's death. I despaired that we would descend into anarchy. I despaired that we would forget our laws and our traditions. I despaired, at the thought that our country might never again be a kingdom."

"Today I despair no longer. After laborious research, I have determined that House Lissesul survives—to this day!"

Shocked silence, then a rising murmur as everyone started talking. Meerwen and I were the only ones not speaking, but then she said, "Is this true? Did you know about this?"

"Only… this… week…" I said, and Valandil said, "And that's not all. Ladies and gentlemen, there is a member of the royal family *in this very room!*"

There was a crash. I turned and saw Elrond in his guild robes. He'd dropped a bottle of his best peach champagne. Valandil was still speaking:

"Imagine my surprise when the heir to the throne turned out to be *my own apprentice!*"

Everyone turned to me, the incoming journeyman in his white formal robes. I hunched over, dripping sweat, and hugged myself as if it would do anything. I wasn't much to look at.

"Ladies and gentlemen, I present Prince Angrod, formerly of House Veneanar, but now rightfully recognized as a true son of House Lissesul. Starting today, a new age dawns on the First Realm!"

Meerwen backed away from me in shock.

Then everything went to hell.

"Aaargh!"

I fell to my knees, my stomach burning. I was mortified. Much as I didn't want to be a prince, this was no way to come out as one. My guts turned to ice and my brain to flashing lights. I slumped to the ground, the world smelling like shit and blood. Blinking furiously, I rolled onto my back and thrashed. My vision juddered and my arms flailed. I was reminded of the fish I'd caught the other day. Foam bubbled from my mouth. Gods, what a way to start a dynasty.

"Stay back, folks," Meerwen said. "I've got this under control."

After a thousand years the fireworks in my brain went dark. Then the smoke cleared. I started coming back to myself. Everything was still shaky but I had enough motor control that I could push myself up.

"You all right?" she asked.

I smiled weakly. "I'll be fine. S'just stress."

Then the PAIN hit me. I arched my back so much I stepped on my own head.

"AAAArrruugrch!"

I bit through my tongue. The inside of my mouth tasted coppery, and sweet. My skin bubbled, at least it felt like it was bubbling, each blister full of scalding pus. I'd have clawed my face off if I had motor control. I was screaming, howling, smashing my head on the cold marble floor. Anything to black out on the tearing in my guts.

After nine million years the white-hot nails withdrew and I got my body back. I blinked, and I could see. I'd puked my guts, and what had been expensive grub was now just a smelly puddle on my face.

"Angrod?" Meerwen said. "You're going to be okay."

The wings tore out the back of my suit.

If you've ever spent an hour with your elbows on a table, then leaned back and stretched your arms, you'll know what it felt like. Only this was happening to a third pair of limbs halfway down my back. Felt completely natural, as if I'd had them all my life. A bit like hands, if the fingers were stretched and leathery. The skin was pink and shiny with blood.

This wasn't the last of my problems.

Just when I was trying to stand, something forced me down. I fell to my hands and knees—the marble floor cracked beneath me. The seamless marble floor cracked, as if I'd gained hundreds of times my own weight.

"Angrod? *Angrod?*"

"G-get away, Meerwen. Get away!"

I was growing, but my torso was growing faster. My clothes were being shredded, of course, but then so was my skin. My eyelids and mouth stretched as much as they could, then tore at the corners. My arms grew so long the skin split at the elbows—it looked like I was wearing gloves of my own skin. Glistening underneath were hard white scales.

"What's happening to me?!"

I shuddered, my muscles tensing and twitching. I bulged out of my clothes, the muscles swelling like boils. They flexed, breaking bones and tearing tendons. My bones knit together and then snapped apart. Knit together and snapped apart. Did I mention the pain? No?

"*Aaeeeaarghaarhraa* help meee!"

I writhed on the floor, stretched on the rack of my own body. The guests had fallen back in horror. People were screaming, men and women were pushing for the exits. Meerwen stood her ground, but her hands had turned into fists.

"Oh, gods!" I said through a mouthful of fangs. My jaws jutted forward and I was growing a snout. It poked through my stretched lips—my fucking nostrils were poking through my lips. My scalp was pulled down my neck and down my back. My tail lashed the air. My pants exploded, and then my shoes. I took a moment to mourn my shoes—I'd bought them just for the party. It rained bloody toenails before the talons forced their way out.

Everything went black. I shook my head, and then everything looked different. Everyone glowed in their own personal mana pool, but the ambient magic still streamed into me. *Me!* My body sucked up all the loose energy—enchantments failed across the city. Lights flickered, as transmutation spells stopped turning lard into illuminating gas. Scrying pools collapsed, cutting off communications and splattering their users. At the buffet table, all the desserts began to slump.

My last thought when I blacked out was, *At least I don't have to be king anymore.*

Chapter 9

I opened my eyes and heard the screaming. People were streaming out the doors and diving from the balconies and into the gardens. Odd, that.

The second thing I noticed was that everyone was smaller. Here I was, on all fours, and still I towered over them. The ceiling was closer too, and I made a note to avoid the chandeliers. Whose idea was it to hang them so low? Fucking dwarves.

The third thing I noticed was how angry I was. "Sssonofabitch-onofabitch," I rumbled. I twisted my neck back and forth (this was easier) and took in the scene. The two elder Elanesses seemed rooted to the ground. Valandil gazed up at me, mouth slack.

"What are you looking at?" I said.

"You seem to have turned into a dragon."

"What? That's ridiculous. You've been hitting the maple-sherry gelato, haven't you?"

"That's not the point. The point is that you're a dragon now."

I stood up straight. It wasn't as easy as I remembered, and I had to grab onto a nearby a railing. I looked at it—my claws hooked around a second-floor balcony.

"See what I mean?" Valandil said.

"Whatever. I've always been tall. And how am I talking? Dragons never had lips or vocal cords."

"Notice how your lips aren't moving? That's because you don't have any."

I gnashed my teeth, a sound that filled the hall. I noticed I was using magic to talk—a variant of the voice-amplification spell. "Still doesn't prove a thing."

"What about your wings?"

"I've always had them. Since I was a hatchling, in fact."

"Somebody's in denial," Findecano said. His wife clung to him.

"Hey, hey, nobody's in denial. So I look a little different in some areas. Big deal. I've been under a lot of stress. So my skin's a little weird and everybody looks like food. Haven't you had one of those weeks?"

"Angrod, you're a dragon," Meerwen said.

"Not you too!"

I got down on all fours—I always think better that way. I looked around. "Where'd everybody go? The night is still young." I blinked, then shook my head. "Look, if I were a dragon I would be able to breathe fire, right? And I'm damn sure I can't. Never could. Not even after that time I ran away with the circus."

Findecano and Tari slowly edged off the stage.

My thoughts drifted, but then the wind changed and I was back on course. I remembered I was angry, fucking *furious*, and it was suddenly a good idea to see if I could breathe fire.

I turned to my master. "Make a fool of me, would you?" I stabbed a claw in his direction. "I'm onto your game, old man. This is nothing but an elaborate jest, starting with that nonsense about me being a prince."

Part of me thought this was wrong, all wrong, but another part was shouting *fight fight fight*. I was drunk with anger and maybe rum balls, because who counts cookies, even if they're alcoholic cookies? I stalked closer to the stage. "Did you think you could make me do something I didn't want? I am not your pawn, little man. You have pushed me one square too far."

Findecano's hand lashed out, but the local magic field was completely depleted. Sparks escaped his fingers, but that was all.

I turned to him. "You thought to burn me with your pathetic cantrip?" I growled. "It is I who will burn *you*."

I reared, triangulating on him and his mate. I gathered my breath and waited for them to twitch. Tari blinked, and I threw my head forward and spat white-hot plasma.

Several things happened at once.

The Lord Governor turned to shield his wife, for all the good it would do. Meerwen tackled me around the neck, but without her magic she only weighed as much as any elf girl.

As the plasma left my mouth I thought, *Shit, I really AM a dragon.*

And Valandil Telerunya, former royal adviser and my mentor, stepped into the line of fire with his arms outstretched. With the last of his power he shielded the two people behind him, giving them time to tumble off the stage. Then his magic failed and he died instantly. At least, I hope so. His skin boiled off, his flesh turned black, and his skeleton fell apart. I was a gigantic blowtorch—*nothing* could stand before me.

Four combat mages came in through the skylights and smashed into the ground around me. They must've come in high, gathered their energies, and dropped through the no-magic zone with full mana reserves. They crackled with power. But then, so did I.

While the glass still rained down, the first magician started with the classic fireball—hits like a rock, explodes like a bomb, and burns like napalm. But I twisted my head and it flew past.

BOOM. The magician on the other side hit me with another fireball, rocking me sideways. My scales weren't even singed.

"Did you just attack a fire-breathing dragon with *fire?*" I said. "That's like attacking a polar bear with snowballs, isn't it?"

I lashed out with my claws, caught the first black mage, and bit his head off. The third mage hit me with a blast of cold and the fourth turned the floor to quicksand.

"Hey, not fair!" I said. My paws scrabbled for purchase and my wings flapped for lift but the cold had sapped my strength and I sank under the surface. The marble closed over me and became solid again.

"Did we get him?" said one of the mages.

—I burst out of the ground, flapped my wings, and leaped straight up, crashing through the dome and trailing chandeliers on my wings.

Dragons used to be such a mystery.

For one thing, how could they have six limbs? There's no precedent. No reptile in the fossil record has so many legs. And how could they fly? They were too big, too heavy, and they certainly didn't have the breastbones for it.

Yet here I was, a dragon, and I wasn't just flying—I was flying fast.

Turns out dragons are thaumavores, or magic-eaters. They feed like other animals but also derive sustenance from the ambient energy. Flying, for instance, was possible through air magic. I wasn't even flapping my wings. My body was taking in magic as it came to me, then blasting it behind me for propulsion, like some kind of air-breathing rocket. Wings swept back, I made good time.

Holy balls, what did I just do?

We finally got rid of that meddlesome old man.

Who ARE you?

The dragon Cruix, at your service. Rather, in my own service, as no elf is my master. The mental voice seemed to mutter. *Disgusting ephemera, cluttering the world with your towns and your cities... We should have wiped you out the minute you arrived...*

Who's WE?

Why, we dragons! The rulers of this world! Where have you been, that you have not heard of us?

Those were your thoughts I was thinking, wasn't it?

There was a pause as I allowed him to go through my memories. Now that we knew about each other, our minds had formed divisions. So far the barricades were holding.

Am I the only one? he said, after what seemed like hours. *Am I the only dragon in the world? Am I the last of a proud race, greatest in wisdom and in majesty? Is there no one else?*

Tough luck, buddy.

Things were looking up. Cases of possession weren't unheard of and there were doctors who specialized in them. It would be simple enough to turn around, turn myself in, and turn back to normal. I adjusted my wings, determined to do just that—and continued on a straight path. What the fuck?

I know what you're thinking, little elf, and I will not allow it. I am no mere demon or thoughtform to be banished so easily. I AM A LIVING MIND and I remember the magics of my people. If you try to seek medical care, I will stop you.

This is terrible!

Ah, but it gets worse, at least for you. You see, this situation cannot hold. Two minds cannot share the same head for long. There can only be one outcome, and I tell you this because you have no hope of stopping it.

What happens? TELL ME.

In less than forty days, I, Cruix, shall take over this body and extinguish its original personality. You, Angrod, shall cease even to be a memory.

I was still reeling from that when the hair on my neck stood up. Turns out I still had hair. It was silky and white and went all the way to my tail. I had a mane and trailing mustachios.

I never thought I'd have to become another species before I could grow a beard.

Now that hair was standing on end. The air smelled weird. I wondered what it was—I jinked right.

BOOM. Lighting split the air.

They'd lain in wait, the combat mages. They'd teleported ahead and hovered along my flight path. Cloaked, I couldn't spot them until they split the night with thunder. They flew alongside now, passing lightning back and forth and missing by inches. They were trying hard to hit me, but I was trying even harder to evade them.

Fire mages dove in, covered in flames and screaming for my death. I dodged the living missiles. As a dragon I was agile in the air. I was halfway built for it, unlike the elven mages. Still they dive-bombed me, harried me with lightning and sleet. The ice crystals were sharp and blinding.

Persistent little monkeys, aren't they? Why don't we show them who REALLY rules the skies?

I was about to say no, but then a fire mage singed my moustache. "Okay, that is it!"

I was among them like a hound among rats. I tore them from the sky, bit them in mid-air, and crushed them in my talons. I was bigger, faster, more heavily armed. Those caught in my wake lost power and tumbled from the sky. I almost pitied them.

Stop! Stop! You're killing them!

Isn't this what we want? Finally, power enough to shake the world!

Staaahp!

You're no fun.

Meerwen soared. Her enhanced eyesight gave her a complete view of the battlespace. She grimaced at each casualty. Many of them she knew by name, and it hurt to see them fall. It was clear that Angrod had become a monster. She watched as he tore through the last of the mages. She had to increase speed to keep up.

Part of her wept at the turn of events. Things had been so promising. She couldn't understand how he could be a prince, let alone a dragon. Both princes and dragons had passed from the world before she was born. To hear her father tell it, the world was better for it.

Thinking of the death toll that had begun at the royal palace, she had to agree. Prince or not, Angrod had to die.

The mages were far behind. The dragon was keeping a straight course. She couldn't keep flying much longer —the spell was extremely taxing. It was time.

She cancelled her forward thrust and began to stoop. She held her fists out in front of her and called upon the power of the earth. She was high in the sky, but she'd always had an affinity for the earth and the wind resistance ceased to be a problem as her weight multiplied. She became denser, much denser, and soon was as rigid as a statue.

Down she dived, down and down, gaining speed and power. She poured energy into her earth discipline, and apart from a few course corrections she dropped like a rock. An extremely dense rock, plummeting so fast her skin grew hot. She held her fists in front of her and aimed for Angrod.

I was congratulating myself for the skirmish when something hit me in the back. I stopped feeling my legs. Something wet slithered across my belly.

What was that?

I chanced a look. Oh, shit.

There was a hole in my back, and a bigger one in my abdomen. Whatever had hit me, it had punched all the way through. I was trailing my own guts.

I noticed we were losing altitude.

What do I do?

Do? There is no 'do.' Only DIE.

Chapter 10

Findecano directed the guards as they picked through the wreckage. Overall, it could have been worse. There were plenty of bruises and scrapes among his guests (the dwarven ambassador sprained his ankle jumping onto the garden, the clumsy lump) but there was just one civilian fatality.

Too bad about Valandil. The old fool had been a hero at the end, but it was probably for the best. If his apprentice hadn't killed him, Findecano's man would have. The Lord Governor reflected on the turn of events, trusting on instinct to show him the way.

A healer approached. "Help you with that burn, milord? You shouldn't even be on your feet."

He waved her away. "I'll be fine. Take care of the others. Is my wife going to be all right?"

"They've finished setting her arm. I think that's her walking toward us."

Tari had her arm in a sling. Findecano embraced her, gently. "I'm glad you're okay."

"A clean break and the healer didn't see any other problems. It's a good thing you were on top of me."

He grinned. "I've heard that before."

She punched him with her other arm. "And what about your burn, my husband? That looks bad."

Findecano's right leg was a big mottled burn. It was red, black, and thoroughly seared. The woollen hose was completely gone.

He gritted his teeth. "I'm warding off the pain with air magic. It's not helping it heal, but it'll do until the emergency passes."

The healer had gone. Tari waved her hand and enveloped them in a bubble of quiet. "And how does this affect us?" she said, moving her lips as little as possible.

"It seems I'll have to kill Angrod after all. I was going to have his claim thrown out of court—it was a joke after all—but this has forced my hand."

"I'll wager your agent is pleased with this development."

"Oh, I'm sure. Aren't you, my dear agent?"

"Son of a bitch," said a disembodied voice.

"May I assume that was a general and rhetorical *son of a bitch?* Or were you referring to me?"

The spy fidgeted. "Uh, of course it wasn't you, milord. It's just that I was trying so hard."

Findecano nodded. "Reinforcing the floor under you was a step in the right direction, but you were still a drain on the local magic field. Is there something you wanted to tell me?"

"Just got a message from the Grand Master. He says reports of the dragons' extinction were exaggerated and wishes to tell you he's sending a team to deal with this last one."

"Who told him about it?"

"Uh, I did, milord. But you didn't order me not to."

Findecano frowned. "We're going to talk about your loyalties. In the meantime, tell the head of your order that he may hunt this dragon so long as he doesn't hamper my own efforts. No doubt the public will want the dragon's head."

"He seemed to know all this already. He probably has other assets in the city."

"We'll talk about this later. My dear? Please drop the screen. I must coordinate the cleanup."

Tari dispelled the working and the sounds of the hall rushed in. To Findecano, the many subdued conversations sounded like a military camp after a battle. The spy bowed, invisible to everyone else, and left.

"That man concerns me," Tari said.

"A nice enough boy, for an assassin."

Her eyes widened. "Surely you're not going to introduce her to Meerwen?"

He scratched his chin. "There's an idea. At least he won't transform into a dragon."

They walked over to the mage who'd lost his head. He lay in a body bag. The plastic was too flat above the shoulders.

"Did you know him?" Tari asked.

"Feniel Tarhassdorien. I handled his exit interview. I'm going to have to call his mother."

She reached over and squeezed his arm. "These things happen."

He shook his head. "I thought our generation was the last to deal with dragons. They're damn hard to kill. I would've stopped Meerwen, but she ran out so quickly. Now she's—"

"Mother! Father!"

Meerwen hobbled in, supported by a pair of royal guardsmen. She shook free and moved to hug her parents. "I'm so glad to see you both!"

"Why are you all muddy?" her mother asked. "You've ruined that dress!"

Meerwen grinned. "I did the old bullet drop, punched a hole in the dragon. Splashed into a lake, had to pull myself out of the lake bottom."

"Did you kill it?" her father asked.

She shook her head. "It flew on. We haven't found its body."

"Milord," said Findecano's secretary. "I'm swamped with messages from the city council. They demand action against this rogue wizard or dragon, whatever Angrod Veneanar has become."

"I'm already making a list of the mages and knights that will be on the task force."

Meerwen saluted, thumping her chest with her fist. "My Lord Governor, I formally request to lead that force."

"You, my daughter?"

"I am an officer of the royal guard, and as a mage and knight I'm qualified to lead both warriors and wizards."

Findecano scratched his chin. On one hand, this was a chance to gain more glory for House Elanesse. On the other hand, this was his baby girl.

"Sire, this dragon *must* be hunted down," she said.

"The dragon has a name, remember?" Tari said. "Have you forgotten that he's the reason you're wearing a low-cut gown?"

Findecano coughed. "Is there anything else?" he asked his secretary.

The blonde elf glanced at her notes. "You're under considerable pressure from various special interest groups, all of them demanding action. One such group, BADD, is baying for the dragon's blood."

"BADD?" Meerwen asked.

"Bothered About Dangerous Dragons."

I woke naked and in a hole.

It says something about an elf's drinking habits that I didn't see anything wrong with either of that. I ached all over, and I needed to use magic to soothe my joints and muscles. Again, that was to be expected.

I was in a forest, but for some reason the earth was torn up to one side. As if something had crashed, skipped, and crashed again, ploughing up the ground as it went. Trees had been knocked down, and the ones bordering the clearing were branchless and splintered.

I'd forgotten something. I looked down at the hole. It was shaped vaguely like… what…?

Oh, hell.

I'd done that! I'd turned into a dragon and *murdered* my master. I'd also fought several combat mages and killed a few. I was perversely proud of that, but then I despaired. Valandil, a man I'd known for twenty years, was dead by my hand. So were others.

If that weren't bad enough, there was an alien mind in my head and it would extinguish me in less than three months. To say I was in big trouble would be the understatement of the century. I was twice damned, twice condemned.

On the bright side, they probably didn't want me as king anymore.

It took two hours to find a road. I was somewhere on the Green Plains, roughly between Drystone and the southernmost city of Vergath. I'd flown farther than I thought.

Thankfully, I was no longer naked. Say what you will about our drinking habits, but elves come prepared. I'd tucked a set of clothes into hammerspace. Granted, the thin shirt and boat shoes weren't the best for a midnight hike, but I'd packed them against waking up in a strange bedroom. Who knew I'd be leaving the city via dragon? It certainly wasn't in my horoscope.

Leo: Forces internal and external have put you in a dangerous spot. Maintain control over yourself or risk causing a scene. Now is not the time to debut an outrageous new look.

It was a clear night, with a full moon, and I had my Sight working to make sure I didn't trip on anything. Everything was sparkly, but there wasn't a farmhouse in sight.

There wasn't any sign of pursuit, but that made sense. Flying is tremendously draining if you don't have wings. Also, there were no patrols this far from any city. I was counting my other blessings when—

"Stand and deliver!" a man boomed.

Shit.

The man stepped onto the path. From his voice, size, and manner of dress he was obviously human.

Humans. There was no mistaking them. Six feet tall, heavily muscled, and armed to the teeth. And that was just the women. This character towered a full head and shoulders over me. He was broad, massive, and decked in fur and leather.

"Hand over the valuables!" he said, slapping his side so I could see the longsword on his hip. "Come on, be quick about it!"

"Have you taken a look at me? I've only got the clothes on my back."

"I'll have none of that! I know you elves—you all carry pots of gold and cookies."

Let's kill him, Cruix said.

"Shut up, you bloodthirsty animal!" I said.

"Hey!" The man looked hurt. "This is a legitimate economic transaction. Just cough up some coins and you'll be on your way."

Regular or extra-crispy?

I gritted my teeth. "I've had a really bad day. Please step aside."

"I can't do that."

"Fine." I reached behind me and pulled out my sticks.

The man drew his sword, but hesitated. "Is that all you've got?"

I twirled them, but he didn't seem impressed. "I have spent twenty years mastering the sword," he said. "It would be dishonourable to use that skill on an unarmed man."

"Hey, I *am* carrying weapons!"

He shook his shaggy head. "That won't do."

"Another time, then?" I tried to slip past him but he blocked me with the outstretched blade.

Why don't we— I silenced Cruix with an effort of will. It was easier now that I was an elf again.

"If you give me your word not to run away, I shall make the fight more equal," said the highwayman. Since the alternative was to kill him, I nodded.

He went to a nearby tree, where he selected a straight branch and hacked it free. Trimming off the twigs, he fashioned a staff as long as his sword.

"Now we are ready to fight," he said, holding the staff in a low guard.

The moon was high and bright, but I asked whether he would need additional light.

"That will not be necessary," he said, and I saw his own eyes flash. Oh, right. Humans have catlike night vision.

We attacked at the same time, our weapons splitting the air. Stick met staff met stick. We parried and swung. Our weapons clacked—they clattered and cracked. He had a double reach advantage (longer arms and longer weapon) but I was dual-wielding. And the first rule when fighting a dual wielder is *Watch both hands.*

He parried my strike, went for a rib shot. I batted it aside and snapped a cut at his head. He grunted. He jabbed with the staff and I twisted aside and let it pass. Then I drummed on his chest. Bam-bam-bam.

He rallied and swung the staff down, nearly knocking the stick from my hand. The hand went numb. Damn, he was strong! I peeked at his aura looking for magical enhancement, but he was just naturally powerful. He swept low and I blocked just in time—the staff cracked against my knee and I howled and hopped away.

"Do you yield?" he asked.

"Like hell!"

I came in high, smashing his guard down and jabbing into his chest. It was like poking a tree. He grunted, but whirled the staff one-handed. I ducked the long-range attack. He went on the offensive and the staff seemed to twist and bend. He jabbed and caught me in the gut, knocking the wind out of me. He was good. I threw a stick. He ducked, but it gave me time to get inside his swing. He brought up the staff but it thumped against my upper arm. I grabbed one of his wrists and used my other stick to beat him around the head.

He snorted like a bull and butted me in the chest, then surged forward, hitting me with his shoulder and sending me flying. I'd opened a few cuts in his head but he was very much in the fight. Skilled *and* tough.

Time to cheat. I pointed the stick at his face and triggered a concussive blast. The gust of wind hit like a punch and was my favourite sparring trick.

The runes on my stick flared red and what hit the man's face was a blast of *fire*. "Aaargh!" he said, and dropped his staff.

"Damn! I didn't mean to do that!" I dropped my stick and rushed to his aid, only to get a haymaker to the jaw.

Things went black for a second. I don't remember hitting the ground, but the next thing I knew I was trying to sit up.

"Ugh," I said, turned my head, and threw up. I wondered what I was vomiting when I'd emptied my guts at the royal palace. I decided not to think about it.

"I can still hear you," the man said. "You still want to fight?"

I shook my head, which only made me dizzier. "You won this one, champ."

"You blinded me," he said. "That's no victory."

Slowly I got to my feet. "How about a draw?"

He faced me, then sighed. "I guess that's as good as it gets."

"Did I really blind you?"

"I will heal, in time. Meanwhile I shall be helpless. I won't be waylaying anybody."

"Let me take a look. I know some healing magic and I can have you back on the highway in no time."

He was quiet for a second. "You are a wizard, sir?"

"Journeyman mage."

"So you could have ended this fight before it even started?"

"Uh, yes," I said. Also, I could've just teleported past him. I was in unfamiliar ground, but I could probably have blinked ahead and gotten a head start. Why didn't I think of that?

Heh.

Goddamn dragon. I turned my attention to the human, who now sat with his sword in his hands. "I'm not meant to be a thief, am I?"

"Not in Brandish," I said. "Look, I'm sorry about the flame attack. I honestly just meant to knock you out. I can fix it. Call it my one good deed for the day."

"I am called Heronimo, stranger, and I am in your debt."

Chapter 11

E lves base their magic on the elements of Earth, Air, Fire, and Water, even though those things don't have any scientific basis. When an earth mage imagines they're drawing power from the earth, they're accessing the same energy field as the air mage who's supposedly drawing power from the air. A fire mage doesn't really need a hair-trigger temper, either, and a water mage doesn't need a tub of water, but it helps to associate magic with something. An invisible energy field is, by definition, hard to visualize. It may surround and penetrate every living thing but it's nothing on which to build a belief system.

There are many more elements (such as hydrogen and helium) but we stick to the classics because they relate to a mage's *personality*. Also, helium magic would be ridiculous.

You can tell a magician's elemental specialty by how they look and act. Earth magicians are built solidly and the serious ones go barefoot. Air magicians move fast and talk too much. Fire magicians are famous for their enthusiasm in general and their tempers in particular. And water magicians are, I don't know, caring?

I realized that water magic wasn't my strongest suit, but by then I was already passing my hand over Heronimo's eyes. "Are you feeling any warmth?" I asked.

"Well, there was the fireball…"

"Nevermind." I concentrated on directing the healing energies according to the morphogenic field I'd superimposed over his face.

You need to know anatomy to be a healer. You also need to care about your patients. Well, I'd taken a few art classes and felt bad about blinding the man.

"It tingles," he said.

A healer can't turn dead matter into living matter—that's hundreds of times more difficult. However, a good one can seal wounds, purge infections, and regulate body functions. A master water mage can even shapeshift.

Healing eyeballs is delicate work, but my efforts were having some effect.

"I'm starting to see… but everything's so dark… wait, it's still night."

Slowly I got the swelling down. The blisters receded. I undid the damage on a cellular level and Heronimo blinked. Then he added his own powers.

Humans might not be as long-lived or as magically-talented, but they make up in other ways. They're big, strong, and hard to kill. They can eat almost anything and live in virtually any climate. Many humans make a point of wearing nothing but leather loincloths or fur bikinis, even in winter.

They do it because they can. And to be honest, if I had those kinds of muscles I'd want to show them off too.

Humans also have a healing factor. It's inborn, doesn't require training, and works whether they're thinking about it or not.

"How does it look?" Heronimo asked.

"Pretty good," I said, helping him to his feet. "You won't need to trim your eyebrows for a while, though"

"I'm hungry," he said.

"That's normal."

"No, I'm *really* hungry. When I arrived in Brandish, I expecting to live by banditry. But brigands do not thrive here."

"What did you do up north?"

"Mostly I chopped wood and carried water."

"In the First Realm, most travellers don't have much cash. Not with the Bank of Brandish in every town. And for everywhere else there's Mithish Card."

Heronimo's stomach rumbled.

"Is there an inn around here?" I asked. "I'm hungry too. Let's walk."

"I'm confused. Do elves have no use for silver or gold?"

We were walking down the road, hopefully toward food and shelter. I looked up at him. "We do have gold and silver coins. We call the silver coin the *rupee*, and we mostly use it for overseas trade. It's just too easy for earth mages to adulterate them with cheaper metals. Within the kingdom, we use folding money."

"So elves use leaves for money? I thought it was an old bard's tale."

I took out my money clip and peeled off a single. "Here you go."

He took the bill and held it up to the moon. "This is money? What're all these pictures?"

"That's one sov'rin. The building is the royal palace and the old man on the other side is our last king, Galdor Lissesul. Stern-looking geezer, isn't he?"

"He looks like you, but older."

"He does not! There's not enough light. And all elves must look the same to you."

"I can see clearly, thanks to you, and I have a good memory for faces. There's one that I shall never forget —the face of the elf that killed my parents."

It was the hottest time of the year. That wasn't much in the Northlands, but at least river bathing was an option. All you needed was soap, a towel, and a hammer.

Something was taking the men of the village. They had begun disappearing during the night, their bodies later found without their skins—or worse. Something was butchering the warriors and taking trophies from their bodies. The chief sent out his finest trackers, but nothing returned from the forest, not even the hounds.

Then Heronimo's father, Hrascar, spoke to the chief. "Let all of us men gather in the great hall," he said. "Let us lie in wait for this monster and kill it together." The chief agreed and they bedded down in his house.

Although Heronimo had not yet undergone his initiation, he ran to his father and demanded to be included. His father tousled the boy's hair. "Sorry, son. This is for warriors only."

"I'm almost nine! I *will* be a warrior!"

"You shall, but not today. Stay with your mother and keep her safe."

"But I wanna see the monster!"

"When this is over we'll hang what's left of it from the gates. How's that?"

The boy sniffled. "You promise?"

"I promise."

The young Heronimo ran off. He got his wooden sword and played with the other boys. Bones were broken and blood was spilled, but no more than usual.

Night came and the entire village lay awake in their beds, ears straining to catch the slightest sound. They heard dogs, cats, and even mice, but of the monster there was nothing. In the morning they stumbled into the light, eyes red and heads numbed. Nobody had died, however, and the chief declared it a good enough plan to be worth trying again.

The next night, the same thing happened: Exactly nothing.

And the next night.

And for an entire week after.

At that point, people were secretly wishing that somebody would die, if only for a change of pace.

Heronimo was playing outside the stockade when the crone appeared. She was shrivelled and bent, with more wrinkles than pores. She carried an odd bundle and peered at him with her one good eye. She cackled.

The boy screamed and ran. He returned with his mother, Grimalda, who asked the old woman what she thought she was doing.

"Just passing through. Thought you might want to see what I've got here." She opened the bundle and revealed a wyvern head. "Found this beauty dead in the mountains. Its nest was lined with swords, spears, axes, knives. Reckon it rolled over too enthusiastically, cut itself, and died from infection. It was bloated when I found it—it *popped* when I stuck me knife in."

"Ew," Grimalda said. "But why cut off its head?"

"There were also human bones in the nest, fresh ones. Reckon it went insane for shiny things and started killing for them. Have you been missing warriors?"

"Gods. This must be it!"

She took the old woman to see the chief. The warriors looked at the wyvern head and nodded among themselves. Wyverns were more than dangerous enough, they liked shiny things, and it was possible for one to prey on people. It looked like they had their monster.

The chief yawned and nodded. "Old woman, you have done this village a service. What would you ask of us?"

The crone cackled, as crones are wont to do. "I have no need of treasure. Only, if someone would escort me to the next village I would be grateful."

"I will do that," said Grimalda.

"But Ma!" Heronimo said.

She smacked him upside the head. "It's only half a day's journey. I should return this evening."

He watched her mother leave with the crone. He forgot about them when his father nailed the wyvern head to the village gates.

The chief had ordered a party in honour of the fallen warriors and in celebration of the fact that the monster was dead. Hogs were butchered and set to roasting. Sheep were slaughtered and set to stewing. Cakes were battered and set to baking. All manner of things were deep-fried. Children ran from house to house, stealing from the kitchens. The village was hip-deep in festivities by the time Grimalda returned.

"Hello, Ma," Heronimo said as she came in through the gates. "Did you bring me anything from your trip?"

"What? No, I hurried home as soon as I could."

He watched as she went into the storeroom. It happened that Grimalda was the village brewer, and famous for her meads and ice beers. She emerged with a keg of honeyjack.

"That's your best stuff! Are you just going to give it for free?"

She smiled. "It's a party. I'm going to give everyone a cup."

"What, even the slaves?"

He watched his mother distribute the distilled mead. She made sure to give everyone, including the children, but Heronimo stayed away. Something was wrong.

The people danced and laughed and, more often than not, swilled honeyjack. In the mead hall his father did backflips over the table, the chief and his warriors exchanged poetic insults, and the bard sang outrageous lies.

People began dropping.

Still singing, the bard stumbled into the fireplace and didn't get up. Women screamed, staggered, and slumped. Children curled up where they fell.

The chief drew his sword and called to arms, but a fireball came from nowhere and blew his head off.

The warriors grabbed and spears and tried to get into formation but the fireballs kept coming. They shot from the rooftops, they shot from the windows, they shot from the rafters and shadows. Those who hadn't fallen to poison died by fire. When only a handful of men remained standing, something hit the floorboards and began shredding them.

Heronimo was under a table. His father had his sword out. He reeled from the honeyjack but was still in the fight. He charged at the thing but it avoided him. It seemed to be made of blades. His comrades fell and still it eluded him.

"Face me, damn you!"

The thing beheaded a warrior. The blood sprayed. Now a red shape danced among the humans, twin blades slashing and killing.

"Face meee!" Hrascar roared.

Then it was just him and the monster. Heronimo's father brought up his sword. "I am Hrascar and you shall die for this!"

The monster giggled. The sound gave Hrascar pause.

The monster let the curtain slide away. The bloody water, now useless as an invisibility cloak, flowed down its legs. It wore a steel fox mask and Grimalda's dress.

"What?" Hrascar said. He lowered his sword as the monster sauntered closer. It made one shark-toothed sabre disappear. It reached up and removed its mask—it was Heronimo's mother.

"Hi honey, I'm home!" she said. She closed the distance and opened his throat with a sawing motion, cutting deeply into his neck.

Heronimo's father died silently, shocked speechless. The monster watched him bleed and chuckled to herself. "Muscle-bound idiot," she said.

Grimalda wiped her sword on Hrascar's shirt. Her features softened, melted, and became someone else's. It was an elf. A male elf, as far as Heronimo could tell.

"Very good, apprentice." Another cloak dropped. Another masked elf stood in the great hall. "Cute dress, though."

"Whatever. Do I pass?"

"Certainly. You got all the warriors. Nice touch, poisoning all the villagers. But are you sure you got everyone?"

Heronimo couldn't breathe.

"Quite sure," the apprentice said, but he didn't sound like it.

"Then what is *this?*" Something grabbed Heronimo and threw him between the two. Another cloak dropped and there were three elves in the room.

"What did I tell you about situational awareness?" said the elder elf.

"Failed a spot check," added the third elf.

"Give me a second and I'll take care of this loose end."

The elder elf shook his head. "I'm going to let him go as a lesson to you. Our order demands absolute thoroughness. If you set out to murder an entire village, you better not leave survivors! You show much talent, my apprentice, but also much arrogance. Let this be a lesson in humility."

"Maybe this kid will grow up into a hero," said the third elf. "Then he's going to find you and kick your arse."

"Shyeah, right."

Heronimo glanced from elf to elf. He had long since soiled himself. He looked to the elder elf and fought to keep his voice steady. "Can I go? Where is my mother?"

"Go, little barbarian," said the elder. "Tell your people a single elf did this."

"Go to the next village," said the apprentice. "You will find your mother on the way. Grow into something worth killing."

Heronimo ran, ran from the hall and from the village. He ran from the corpse of his father, from the ruins of his life. He ran for his mother, the last thing in the world. He ran until his legs ached and his lungs burned.

He was halfway to the next village when he saw her. She was hanging from an elm tree.

Chapter 12

Heronimo raised his beer and drank mightily. I, too, had to drink from my own mug.

"That was some story," I said.

"Sorry," he said. "Didn't mean to unload on you."

I shook my head. "S'no problem. Besides, as you'll soon find, I've been through some heavy stuff too."

I signalled to a barmaid for another round. "And can we have some whisky shots too? My friend has never had a boilermaker."

Over the remains of our bread and stew, I quickly filled him in on my situation. Our drinks arrived and I sank the whisky shots into our beers.

"What sorcery is this?" Heronimo said. Not sure if he was serious.

We drank and leaned back. We sat in a booth in the empty dining lounge. Almost everyone was asleep, but inns always had at least one night owl employee to attend to travelling dark elves. The barmaid, a shapely dark elf herself, was currently scrubbing the floor.

I pulled myself away from the view and looked at Heronimo. "So your plan was to eventually mug this murderer?"

He frowned. "Give me some credit. I was only going to live as a highwayman until I had the funds to continue searching. How hard would it be to find an elf that wields a pair of saw-toothed sabres?"

"Dual-wielding is pretty common, actually. Off the battlefield, many elves carry matched personal weapons. Even I have my sticks."

"Yes, that gave me a shock. Then I realized you sound different. Also, you're shorter."

"I'm average height!" I said. "Anyway, I've never heard of a group that wears fox masks."

Heronimo leaned closer and whispered. "This dragon in your head—is it dangerous? Can it hear us?"

"It sees and hears everything. So far it's suggested I enlist you as my minion and burn down the inn. But I've got it under control."

"Like you had that air blast under control?"

I was about to speak, but I shut my mouth. That had been an old spell of mine, and I shouldn't have confused it with another spell, let alone a spell I'd never used before. The mental gymnastics involved in turning a blast of air into a fiery attack were like the ones I used when I was a fire-breathing dragon.

Shit.

"What's your plan, man?"

I buried my face in my hands. I had no idea. And I'd been blissfully unaware until Heronimo asked. My thoughts came sluggishly. I did long division in my head and kept misplacing numbers. I wasn't operating at full capacity—and I thought I knew why.

Feeling around in the back of my head, I found Cruix. He was there, a definite presence. I could imagine him atop my brain, blanketing the gray matter with his wings and digging into the folds with his claws. He had his tail wrapped around my hindbrain.

Suddenly I knew what a dragon hoard felt. And I knew beyond doubt that I was doomed.

"I shouldn't have criticized your plan," I told Heronimo. "I only want is to see my home one last time."

"Must be nice, to have a home to return to."

"Why don't you come with me? My best friend is the best double-sworder in Corinthe. He probably knows your man."

"Will it be easy to get there?"

"It's on the other end of the continent, and we'll have to avoid the main roads for the entire journey. We'll need horses, supplies, and above all money. I can't go to the bank because I'm a wanted man—my account is sure to be frozen."

"With frost magic?"

"Worse. With accountants."

"Excuse me," the barmaid said, "but I couldn't help overhearing."

"Weren't you way over there?" I asked. "How much did you eavesdrop?"

"You're not the first adventurer with a terrible secret. Keep your dark side on a leash and we'll be okay. You need travelling money?"

"Let me guess, you're a princess in disguise."

She stuck out her tongue. "No, but there *is* a dwarven prince in one of the rooms. He's looking to go on an adventure and needs a native guide."

"I'm as native as they come. And Heronimo can be our porter."

"Hey!"

We crashed in one of the basic rooms for a few hours. The barmaid promised to wake us at breakfast so we could meet this prince. She needn't have bothered.

Heronimo and I were snoring in our beds when the door shattered inward and a bearded creature thundered in.

"ARE THESE THE STALWART ADVENTURERS?"

I backflipped out of bed and drew my sticks. Heronimo snarled and threw off his blanket, confirming that humans do indeed sleep with their weapons. We stood poised to defend ourselves, with every nerve and muscle tensed.

"Impressive!" the dwarf said. "The barmaid told me about you, but she neglected to mention what fine-looking fellows you were. I am Minos Magnusson, and I crave *advenchar!*"

Heronimo and I glanced at each other. Dwarves were often boisterous, but there was something strange about this one. He was smaller and younger than usual. Those rosy cheeks hadn't seen their hundredth year, and even in armour he was more cute than fearsome.

Hah, a cute dwarf. So there *was* such a thing.

"I seek a quest to test my mettle," he said. "For that I need companions stout and true."

"Off to see the world, eh?" I said. "Wouldn't you rather stand in a nice garden?"

"What?"

I coughed. "In truth, we are already on a mission. I am Angrod and this man-mountain is Heronimo. He is the mightiest warrior in the Northlands, and completely without fear."

My human friend rolled with the bluff. He lowered his sword and flexed. You could almost hear his skin creaking.

"Heronimo has journeyed from distant lands in search of sweet, sweet *justice*. An elven wizard turned his parents to stone. Even now this cruel wizard evades our grasp!"

"I will rescue my parents, no matter the cost," Heronimo said. "If I must vanquish one hundred foes at once, so be it! I have trained twenty years for such a battle."

"I would be honoured to help!" Minos said, and puffed out his chest. "I have been waiting for such a quest all my life. Have you really been training for twenty years?"

"That's how I got these scars."

I looked at Heronimo. Whoa. I hadn't noticed the previous night, but his entire upper body was a tapestry of wounds. There were long scars, deep scars, straight scars, and jagged scars. There were scars on top of scars *on top of scars*. They covered his arms, shoulders, and chest. I'd never seen anything manlier.

"Humans heal quickly, but in my eagerness to gain mastery of the sword I traded safety for realism. We practiced with red-hot swords."

That was *insane*.

"That is fantastic," Minos said. "When do we leave?"

A fat elf barged into the room. "What's all this? Who's going to pay for this door?" Minos took one look at him and tossed him a gold coin. The innkeeper caught it and waved a hand over it to test its purity. "Yippee! A gold yippee!"

"Indeed," Minos said. "That should more than pay for our bill."

"I'm not sure about Minos," Heronimo said. "I mean, he talks a good talk, but he's also a complete novice."

"We need him," I said. "Without him we wouldn't have all this stuff."

I was referring to our fine new travelling clothes, our palfreys and pack mules, and our supplies. Everything was the best in town.

Minos was across the street, haggling over camping lanterns. Dwarves always seem to get the best bargains, partly because they have the ability to identify magic items, and also because they're heavily into commerce. If they aren't merchants, they're suppliers. Either way, a dwarf gets a discount.

"He's enthusiastic, but not battle-tested," Heronimo said.

I dug into my pocket for the walking-around money our companion had given us. I came up with a handful of silver rupees and one gold yippee. The last was a solid metal oval—it was practically a small ingot.

"A family could live on this for a year," I said. "And he's got more in that bottomless pouch. Never underestimate the power of money."

"Won't that make him a target? I know I wouldn't hesitate to waylay him."

"You might be in for a shock," I said. "I took a peek at his gear. Most of it's magical."

"So? Dwarves always have enchanted items."

"Yes, but the average dwarf only carries one or two. His Highness has over a dozen, and they all shine brightly in my Sight."

Chapter 13

"How wonderful it is, to be out on the open road!" Minos said.

I groaned and shifted in the saddle, trying to take the weight off the sores. It was an excellent saddle on a well-behaved horse, but the problem was with the rider. As a city elf I knew practically nothing about horses. I'd ridden often enough, back home, but that was a long time ago and it hadn't prepared me for cross-country riding.

For one thing, the schedule was running me ragged: Get up an hour before dawn and feed the horses. Have breakfast, break camp, and walk the animals. Mount up when their stomachs had settled. March for five hours, feeding the damnable beasts every hour. Break for lunch. Rest until two in the afternoon, then ride three hours to the next camp. Straight to bed and sleep like the dead.

We managed twenty-five to forty miles a day, five days a week. Distance-wise, it was better than going on foot. Comfort-wise, I'd rather have walked.

To make things worse, I was suffering alone. Heronimo proved to be an experienced tracker and horseman. He was also a good forager and our meals never lacked for fresh ingredients. (He found so many eggs we fed them to the mules.)

Minos was about as outdoorsy as I was, but made up for it in enthusiasm. He had a Belt of Strength and a Ring of Regeneration, which meant he was unaffected by saddle sores or fatigue. The little dwarf was constantly gushing about the fresh air, the wide-open skies, and the unspoiled wilderness. Personally, I could have done without the bugs.

Do you shake out your boots before you put them on? I do now.

Minos also had a crossbow that allowed him to hit anything. You just needed to point it in the general direction and it would shoot at the perfect moment. Thanks to that, we didn't lack for fresh meat either—we fed it to the horses. These were capran horses, and more than a little carnivorous.

We made good time through the Green Plains, but I wasn't in a cheerful mood when we sighted Mount Rasmus, an extinct volcano with a perfect cone and a caldera lake. For all my aches and pains I had to admit it was quite a view.

I remembered there was a small halfling village just past the mountain. Besides catering to tourists, it also raised all manner of fruit in the rich volcanic soil.

"Are we there yet?" I asked.

"Angrod, my friend, you do not enjoy life on the road?" Minos asked.

"I prefer proper beds and indoor plumbing."

Heronimo turned to me. "What is this thing you call *plumbing?*"

"Seriously? What did you use, snow?"

"Actually…"

"Snowball fights must've been something else, huh?"

"Fellows, the village is burning."

We'd rounded a bend in the trail, and we could see black smoke rising from the village below. Even from a distance we could see bodies.

Heronimo squinted. "There's just one building on fire. No signs of life, but I could be wrong."

"I vote we circle around it," I said. "Give it plenty of room. There are other towns on the way."

"And what if there are survivors?" Minos said. "Surely as heroes we cannot ignore our duty?"

"I can ignore it just fine, but…" Heronimo gave me a look.

We rode into the village, into the aftermath of a massacre. Dead halflings were everywhere. Most had been literally cut down, as in with large blades, but a few had that exploded look that comes from fireballs.

"This looks familiar," Heronimo said, and drew his sword.

"We do a quick sweep and then we're gone," I said. "Five-yard spread. No sound."

"Hello, the village! Is anyone alive?" Minos said, bellowing like a bull.

I winced. "Nevermind."

We rode around the village. I kept a glyph on, looking for heartbeats, while Heronimo used his naturally keen senses.

"We're here to help!" Minos said. "Is anyone alive?"

"Like the dead would answer you," I said. Most of the bodies were too mutilated to live.

Halflings have always been a sad race. They were clumsier than elves, not much bigger or stronger, and terribly short-lived. Few were lucky enough to live a hundred years. Worst of all, they had no magic whatsoever. To see so many cut down, in what passed for the prime of their lives... What could do this?

"I'm not getting anything," Heronimo said.

"Me neither," I said.

The burning hut collapsed. We started at the sound, but then we heard the weeping.

"Over there!" I said, pointing at a stone cottage. We rode up and dismounted. Heronimo was the first one in, stepping over a corpse to get through the door.

Huddled in a corner was a halfling boy no more than ten years old. He stared at us, then hissed.

"It's all right," Heronimo said, in the same voice he used with horses. "We're not here to hurt you. What's your name? Where are your parents?"

The boy just stared. He hadn't blinked since making eye contact. "My parents are dead. They're all dead. I'm the last one. I'm Conrad."

"When did this happen?" Minos asked.

"Yesterday. Haven't slept."

"Well, you can relax," I said. "You're safe now."

"No, I'm not," the boy said. "I'm *not*. And neither are you."

"Rrraargh."

The body at the door stood up. It couldn't have been alive, it was drained of blood—and yet it moved. Moaning, it raised its arms and lurched toward us.

"That was my father."

Minos drew his axe and buckler. I drew my sticks. Everyone looked at me. The boy snickered. "Sticks? These are the undead, not the undrummed."

"If you've got anything better, I'd be glad to take it off your hands."

"Thought you'd never ask," Minos said. He tossed me a flanged mace. "The Mace of Shock."

I caught it by the business end. "Ow!"

The zombie hobbled toward us. Heronimo frowned, told the boy to close his eyes, and stepped forward. The zombie hit the floor in two pieces.

"Awesome!" the boy said.

"I told you not to look!"

"Boys?" Minos said. "There are more of them."

We glanced out the windows—all the dead bodies were on their feet. The men carried farm tools and the women had kitchen knives. Tarlike fluid oozed from every wound. Our horses had already bolted, of course.

"You ever feel you're in the wrong story?" I said.

"AAAAARGH!" Minos said, and charged. He slashed and punched the air.

"After him!" I said, and waded into the fight. I clubbed a zombie with the mace, then pointed with the stick and triggered a concussive blast. It blew another zombie to flaming bits.

"Wow!" the boy said. He picked up a rock and threw it.

Heronimo walked up to a zombie, cut it in half, walked up to another zombie, and did the same thing. He carelessly parried a zombie with a rake, then ran it through. The zombie walked down the blade and rapped him on the head. Heronimo tore his sword loose and chopped it in two.

I glanced at the zombie I'd bashed in the head. It was down. "Go for the head or chop it to bits!"

"Who's a dwarf and a half! *I'm* a dwarf and a half!" Minos said, hacking in all directions. He fought without technique, without skill, but he was strong and fast. He ripped through the zombies and stomped them into mush. "There's nothing my axe can't fix!"

A zombie thrust with a long shovel, but Minos's chain mail turned hard as plate. It lunged and tried to bite him, but he blocked with his buckler and slashed it in the throat. A well-aimed boot forced it back.

The village blacksmith lumbered in, a hammer in either hand.

"You are huge!" Minos said. "That means you have huge guts!" The little dwarf threw himself at the giant.

Something knocked me to the ground—it was a zombie dog. Even the animals were coming back to life. "Aaaugh get it off get it off!"

"I'll save you!" Heronimo said, but was swarmed by undead chickens.

The blacksmith swung his meaty arms, hammers weaving a wall of hurt. Minos backed away, then drew a pistol and shot the zombie in the face. The heavy wooden bullet blew out the back of its head and the zombie tumbled backward.

"Grooveh!" Minos said.

I remembered I was an elf and teleported out of there. I reappeared six feet up and landed on the dog. I rolled off and kicked it in the ribs, then smashed its skull with the mace. I looked to Heronimo. He was walking out of a cloud of feathers.

"Let's not ever talk about this," he said.

The boy whooped and threw more rocks. "Yes! Yes! So much violence!"

"Weren't these your friends and neighbours?"

"That was yesterday!"

Fighting for real, Heronimo was a wonder. In his hands the longsword was lightning quick. He swept his blade and decapitated three at once, then chopped a zombie from neck to crotch. A cut, a parry, and he did the same thing to another zombie, only from crotch to neck. It took a step before falling in two pieces.

Another wave fell on us, but we broke their numbers through sheer ferocity. I turned on my Sight and confirmed that Minos was using magic. His gear blazed with runes. There was a speed spell in his boots and a bloodlust buff in his axe. With so many enchanted items even the boy would be a tough opponent.

Not being a melee specialist, I stayed on the edges, throwing fire where needed. The upgraded spell used only a fraction of the focus needed for a fireball. Instead of gathering water vapour and setting it on fire, it set the *air* on fire. I blasted the zombies from medium range and bashed the ones who got too close.

It was over in minutes. The doubly dead covered the ground. There was no blood, but the sticky black stuff more than made up for it. Everything stank.

"Ugh," I said, and wished for an air-purification spell.

"Urgh," Minos said, and the young dwarf bent over and vomited through his beard.

Heronimo wiped his blade on a corpse's shirt. He glanced at the smouldering remains of the cottage and frowned. "The boy said this village was attacked yesterday. Why was that still burning?"

We all stared at each other.

"It's a trap!"

A fireball came out of nowhere and blew off Heronimo's left arm. "Aagh!"

More fireballs exploded around us, but we were moving too fast. "Run away, run away!" Minos said. We fled the village.

The two assassins on the roof watched them go. They dropped their veils and stretched their legs.

"Told you it wasn't going to work."

"Shut up, Dagonet."

"Working for the Lord Governor has made you soft. And you put *so much effort* into slaughtering this village."

"How was I to know he'd have bodyguards?" the spy said. "A barbarian and a dwarf. Angrod alone would have fallen to the zombies."

"We missed our chance here. Keep following them and I will report to our master."

"You always get the cushy jobs."

"I've always been the clever one. It's not my fault you're bad at everything."

"Say that again. I'd have run you through already if I weren't tired from raising the dead."

"But you *are* tired. While I am well-rested."

"We both know I'd beat you in a fair fight," the spy said. He adjusted his fox mask and glared at Dagonet, who laughed.

"My dear man," Dagonet said, "when has the Elendil Order ever fought fair?"

"Thanks for snagging my arm back there," Heronimo said.

"No problem," Conrad said, and pulled his blanket closer.

Heronimo stretched his left arm. We'd bandaged it tightly but had otherwise done nothing except rinse the stumps and press them together. His healing factor was that good.

We'd caught up with our horses and mules after our undignified retreat, which told us we were fleeing in the right direction at least. After putting the boy on the spare horse, we didn't stop until we had a wide river between the village and us. The horses were exhausted, but at least we could breathe easily.

We camped on the edge of Deepwood, just past the bridge, where we would see if anything tried to cross. I'd set a few magical traps and Minos had put down a sentry crystal that would wake us if anything approached.

We huddled around the fire and tried not to glance at the bridge.

"So my village was just bait?" Conrad asked. "And the real target was *you?*"

I couldn't meet his eyes. "I'm sorry," I said. "If we'd only known..."

"Goddammit to hell. Why did it have to be my village?" the boy said, finally bursting into tears. "We were nobody. We didn't matter. WHY DID IT HAVE TO BE US?"

I reached out, but Heronimo scooped him into a hug. "I'm sorry. I know exactly how it feels."

For long minutes the boy cried into Heronimo's shoulder. No one spoke.

"Why can't we defend ourselves?" Conrad said. "Everybody else has magic. You got your arm blown off and you're all better. It's not fair! It's not fair."

"What would you have me do?" Heronimo asked. "Will you trade your childhood for vengeance? Shall I train you twenty years in the ways of the sword?"

"Eh, that's stupid. If I knew who did it, I'd just sneak up on them and drop a rock on their head."

The look on Heronimo's face was priceless. I covered my mouth. Minos coughed and took the pistols from his belt.

"Conrad, these are yours. Tomorrow I'll teach you to shoot them. I can't bring back your parents, but I *can* give you the means to defend yourself."

Conrad sniffed. "How do they work?"

"That's a dwarven secret. But basically they store magic and discharge it into the ammunition." Minos showed us an example. "See the runes? This one propels the wooden bullet and that one makes it explode on impact."

The bullets were beautifully carved and varnished. The guns themselves were ironwood and steel, with smaller parts in crystal and bronze. Each pistol made as well as any clock, and was about as ornate. Swirling patters were etched into the metal surfaces. Clearly aristocratic weapons.

Guns weren't as good as fireballs—they weren't even as accurate or long-ranged as bows and crossbows. They were a lot more expensive too. Nevertheless, they were a lot better than throwing rocks, and nearly as easy to figure out. I nodded in approval.

Minos leaned back and holstered the pistols. "I'll teach you first thing in the morning. Try to get some rest in the meantime."

We wolfed down a quick dinner and went to sleep.

Chapter 14
Middlegame

I was back in the cave. Cruix was there. We played chess on a stone table. I was steadily running out of pieces.

"Haven't you wondered why I have not spoken?" he asked. "Surely you must have noticed my silence these past few weeks."

"I have been curious, yes."

The dragon smiled with his eyes. He moved another piece. His horns and ventral scales were golden in the light.

"I am content to wait. I have been stuck in a waking dream for *centuries*, so even a passive existence feels liberating. Oh yes, I remember being made of stone. Rocks can think, although not quickly."

I frowned at the board. He had the white pieces and I had the black, but the table wasn't your regular chessboard. His side was completely white, mine was completely black, and pieces could only move on squares of the same colour. The pawns were an exception: They could move on any colour and extend the player's territory with every forward push.

Things were grim for my side. I'd lost my knights, my bishops, even my queen. My king was looking nervous, for a chess piece.

"Frankly, I still don't have much control. Your subconscious has been fighting me every step of the way. Every neuron is a battleground, every synapse a skirmish. I always win, of course, but it's slow."

He moved another piece and I looked around. The cavern was bright thanks to all the candles. Severed hands lay everywhere, palms down, and the candles had been set in holes on the back of each hand.

"I could ask you to surrender. Your consciousness would merge with mine and we would become one." He moved another piece. "But I see no profit there, and I don't believe you'd agree to it either."

"You know me well," I said.

"I've been going through your memories. For example, do you recall how your father smelled?"

My father used to carry me on his shoulders. For a second I remembered the smell of his hair—and it was gone.

"Or what your mother sang to you when you were little?"

A woman, singing softly to herself and to her baby. The song was melancholy sweet. Father must have been gone by then, and Mother would have known she would shortly follow. Elves might not be too fertile, but they stay viable until the end. It rarely happens, but sometimes a couple will have a baby before they die.

A long childhood is one thing. A long childhood without parents is another. I didn't have many memories of them. This one was almost real enough to
—

"But enough of that. How about your first mango?"

Through a mouthful of sweet I said, "You son of a bitch."

He laughed. "You mammals indulge your offspring, don't you? Me, I never knew my sire, and good thing too."

"He was probably your grandfather as well, you misbegotten son of a snake."

The dragon hissed and the candles wavered. "I shall savour the moment your mind dies. I shall keep the memory, even as I do away with every iota of your being."

Then he laughed his evil laugh.

HAHAHAHAHAHAHA

"Angrod, wake up!" Heronimo said, shaking me awake.

"Huh? What? Where?" I said. I sat up and looked around. It was dark and I could barely see. "Was I dreaming?"

"Yes, you were," Minos said. "You woke us up with your laughter."

"Huh," I said.

"Angrod, I've got a question," Conrad said. "Why did you cut our hands off?"

I saw them. Heronimo, Minos, and Conrad. They stumbled forward, reaching with their stumps, darkness oozing from eyes and mouths. "Whyy did you kkill usss?"

"Aauuggh!" I said. "Aaaugh!"

"You okay, Angrod?" Heronimo said. "You were having a nightmare."

I reached over and pinched him.

"Ow! What was that for?"

"If this were a dream, I'd have felt that."

"Fair enough."

It was nearly light, so I fed the animals, made coffee, and waited for sunrise.

When it came, it played over the bridge and I leaned back to appreciate it properly. It was a living bridge. The roots of four massive trees (two on each side) had been trained to grow across the river and take hold on the opposite bank. The roots had been interwoven and the cracks sealed with mud. They had thickened and strengthened. Stepping-stones had been laid along their length.

Such a bridge wasn't just maintenance-free—it would also grow stronger over time. This particular one was easily two thousand years old.

We would be passing through Deepwood, the stronghold of the wood elves. They were friendly enough, if you weren't running from the law. They would certainly detect us, so I rehearsed my bluff.

"Morning," Heronimo said. He had a mug in his hand.

"Morning," I said.

"Minos and the kid are still out. We ought to let them sleep. If I'm not mistaken, that was their first real battle."

"Heh. That was my second real battle, and I wasn't a dragon this time."

Heronimo took a sip. "Can we rely on the Minos's trinkets?"

"The dwarves are excellent artificers, but the spells built into their gear tend to be simple. They can be blocked or counteracted." I sipped from my mug. "They're also useless in a depleted magic field. Actually, even your healing factor would be. How's the arm?"

My friend untied his splint and unwrapped the bandage. He flexed the arm and made a fist. "Just more scars."

The afternoon was pleasant. Minos took Conrad to practice shooting, and Heronimo and I practiced our weaponry as shots echoed along the river.

"Remember, a dual wielder's hands are independent," I said, parrying with the stick, "The off hand will lean toward defence but both can strike or block."

I menaced him with the stick and hammered at him with the mace. "Then again, you can expect magic half the time when you're fighting an elf."

I blinked behind him. He spun around, but I tapped him on the shoulder with the stick, then loosed a concussive blast that forced him to duck. I swung the mace underhanded, but he blocked it with the flat of his blade and went for a close-range stab, gripping the naked blade in one hand.

"Don't you need a gauntlet?"

We stepped apart and he looked at his hand, which healed so fast the blood steamed.

"Not really."

Not to be outdone, I teleported again. It was exhausting, but I managed to tag him with the mace. The electric shock made him jump. I blinked from side to side and fired steam into his face. Of course, I didn't dare do more than harry him because Heronimo was a powerhouse. He could take or dodge most of my spells and I had no doubt he would kill me in a serious fight.

I lunged, mace cocked for an overhead blow, and Heronimo yelled so hard I forgot myself. This allowed him to parry my stick, wrench the mace from my hands, and kick my legs from under me.

I was flat on my back, staring straight up.

"Heronimo, did you by any chance train in a convent?"

"These are amazing trees," Minos said. "I have heard of nothing like them."

We rode down the narrow trail, sunlight filtering through the branches. The trees were all the same kind. Each was a leafy tower so wide you could fit a dance floor in one hollowed-out trunk. Only a little light made it through the forest canopy, and at ground level it was chilly and dark.

"The trail could be wider, though," Minos said. "Surely this place has a tourist trade?"

Conrad shook his head. "An elf-witch lives in these woods. She discourages intruders."

"How does she do this?" I asked.

"Does she enchant those who look upon her?" asked Heronimo.

"Does she whisper into their minds?" asked Minos.

He didn't see the tripwire, but he *did* see the swinging log that hit him in the chest and knocked him off his horse.

"Minos!" Heronimo said. He swung off his horse and ran to our companion, but the ground opened under him and he fell into the pit.

I'd dismounted at the same time—something grabbed my leg and hoisted me into the air.

"She tends to booby-trap the forest," Conrad said.

The blood was rushing to my head. "I could've used that information five seconds ago!"

He shrugged. "She doesn't usually rig the trails. Anyway, they're nonlethal."

"Hah!" Heronimo said. "So these are *nonlethal* wooden stakes?"

"Can't breathe." Minos said.

"Man, you rang like a gong," I said. I teleported out of the snare, but forgot to reorient myself and landed on my head. "Ow!"

Rich feminine laughter echoed through the trees.

"A little help?" Heronimo said. "Kind if pinned here."

I was getting to my feet when I was surrounded by wood elves. They carried bows and boar spears and didn't look friendly, despite all of them being women.

Heronimo pulled himself out of the hole. He was bleeding from a dozen punctures but he sounded more amazed than hurt. "Did I lose too much blood? We seem to have been ambushed by bikini elves."

"I'm seeing it," Minos said. "They should be ashamed!"

More feminine laughter—and then the Witch of Deepwood stepped out of hiding.

She was tall and red-haired. Her age was just starting to show but gravity had been kind. "Looks like we caught ourselves some big 'uns," she drawled. "We eat well tonight, girls!"

"Eep," Minos said, and struggled to sit up.

"Who is your leader?" the Witch asked.

"That would be me," I said.

"Tell me, dear boy, what are you doing in my land?"

The witch fixed her glittering green eyes on me. Suddenly I knew it wouldn't be wise to lie to her. "I'm on the run because I turned into a dragon. My human friend is hunting for the elf that killed his parents and my dwarf friend is in it for the adventure. The kid's with us because his entire village turned to zombies."

"You didn't tell me about the dragon!" Minos said.

"I'm sorry, buddy. But I had it under control, there was nothing you could do, and plausible deniability. Okay?!"

The Witch grabbed me by the face and looked deeply into my eyes.

"Hey, buy me a drink first!" I said. I felt every layer was peel away. The past few weeks flashed before my eyes. Then she let go and I felt like a finished book. There were tears in my eyes. "Goddammit, we just met!"

Seconded! Cruix said.

The wood elves tensed. Bows were drawn and spears readied. The Witch waved them down. "It's okay, they're fine."

"Does this mean you'll let us go?" I said.

"Sure," she said. "Now, can you tell the boy to lower his weapons? They're still pointed at me and my lieutenant."

"Weapons?" Conrad said. He had his pistols out. Half a dozen arrows and spears were pointed at him, but the guns never wavered. "I don't *need* no stinkin' weapons!"

"Do you always wear so little?" Heronimo asked a wood elf.

"Actually, we only put these on when we're expecting guests. Normally we just wear the bottoms."

We rode down the trail, this time with wood elves jogging along.

I'm not referring to different species when I say wood elves and dark elves. Elves come in all colours (many not found in nature) but we're all just one race. Dark elves are a minority who are born nocturnal, white-haired, and moody. Wood elves, meanwhile, are those individuals who have given up city life for the supposedly more natural lifestyle of our ancestors. This involves bows, spears, and hand-woven tops.

"So what do you all do in Deepwood?" I asked the Witch, who jogged (*joggled*) beside me.

"We hunt, fish, and forage," she said, not breaking stride. "There are small clearings where we grow everything else. We have plenty of leisure, and we mostly just enjoy ourselves."

"I see."

"We do lots of socializing… if you know what I mean." She looked up and winked. "We also protect the forest, the largest single organism in the world."

"Didn't see that one coming. Really?"

"Oh yes. All these trees share the same root system, which is *massive*. It's why Deepwood hasn't fallen into

King's Lake despite being mostly sand. The roots hold everything together."

"And how does this organism repay you? Does it act as the repository for the memories of your people?"

"Ah, no. But we do turn its sap into booze."

Chapter 15

T he main settlement was treehouse heaven. Nothing happened at ground level but instead took place twenty, fifty, a hundred feet up. There were platforms, walkways, and apartments among the trees, all shaped out of living wood. As with the bridge, the wood elves had thrown around some serious magic.

Fire magic, oddly enough. The same element that allowed for so much destruction was also helpful in guiding plant growth. This was why nearly every red mage had a bonsai garden.

Going up, there were ladders and spiral staircases. Going down, there were ziplines and ropes. I remembered this was the second reason I'd always wanted to run away with the wood elves. The first reason, of course, was the topless babes.

"Scandalous," Minos said. He practically hissed.

"What's wrong?" I said. "Don't dwarves believe in airing out their nipples? I know humans do."

Heronimo nodded. "Yes, humans boob. I mean, humans do. It's nothing I haven't seen before."

We passed a pair of identical blondes. They had pretty eyes and nice smiles, but that wasn't what held our attention.

"Those two are going to have serious back problems in the future," I said.

"H-how can this be?" Heronimo said. "How can slender elves be so well-endowed?"

"I can see their endowments from behind. They're not even raising their arms!"

"You two are disgusting," Minos said. "And those two are *completely* out of proportion."

Just then I was reminded that wood elves were not a single-gender society.

"Oh my," Minos said. "Oh, my."

The male wood elves were huge—almost as muscular as humans. They lounged about in their g-strings and feathered capes. "Impressive," Heronimo said. "And I thought all elves puny."

"I am not puny," I said. "Give me some light and some posing oil and I'll show you beefcake."

"Angrod, any of these men could break you in half. And while they couldn't do the same to me, I'll admit they would be a challenge."

"The men spend much of their time working on their abs," said the Witch. "Come to think of it, so do the women. We cultivate our bodies, the better to dance and fight. We are not city elves but our lives are full of beauty."

"Art is plumage, eh?" I said. "And here I thought you were just party animals."

The Witch leered. "What better canvas, what better clay, than the artist's own body?"

"No argument," I said. "How about you, Heronimo?"

"Er—"

"We have an hour until dinner," said the Witch, "so make yourselves at home."

"—oh, good. I could use a chance to breast. *Rest*."

"Before there was the moon, there was the earth. Still molten from the forge it was a naked, red, and lonely world. Nothing lived, for nothing made flesh could survive without oceans or clouds. It was a land populated only by impersonal forces. By gigantic elementals that dwarfed the gods. But there were no gods, back when things were new. It was an age of young planets and blind titans. They danced round the sun and flirted with one another.

"One such titan kissed the earth, shattering both worlds. So violent was the force of their coupling that both were shaken to pieces. Our planet survived, but the titan was destroyed. Had you stood on the earth's surface you would have seen horizons meet. The slap would have thrown you into the air even as the ground split and the mountains leaped.

"The world spun like a kicked ball. It rained continents.

"Had you survived, you might have found yourself in the ring of wreckage circling the wounded world. Half the rubble gathered, and over several weeks rock fused with rock and our moon took shape. The other half smashed back to earth. This was iron from the titan's heart. It sank to the planet's centre. This spinning core of molten iron is what throws up the energy that we use in our workings.

"This is the story of the birth of the moon and the origin of magic."

The storyteller bowed. We all applauded. We were in the village square, a platform suspended from four massive trees. Everyone had given something to the buffet table.

"Have you tried these fritters?" Conrad asked. "They're really good!"

"So is the sap-mead," I said. I emptied my cup. "No wonder they protect the forest!"

"Where's Heronimo?" Minos asked. "Wait, I see him… good lord he's gone native."

"Woo!" Heronimo said. He wore little more than tassels and face paint. "I am the ultimate warrior! Fear me, evildoers!"

He ran around the platform and balanced on the railings, pumping his fists and flexing his arms. None of the male wood elves could match him for size or definition.

"Everything about me is larger than life! Everything I have... is *big*."

"Good lord," Minos said, colouring visibly.

"Yeah, the mead sneaks up on you," said the Witch.

Minos was now blushing deeply and I looked closely at the little dwarf. He had a beard, sure, but now that I thought about it—

"Why don't we get out of here?" asked the Witch. "I've got something to show you."

"I bet you do," I said. She led me from the crowd and over to one of the trees, where two ropes awaited us. She handed me one and stepped onto the rail. "You sure you can handle this?"

"I'm an elf!" I said. "I get a dexterity bonus too."

"Okay then," she said, launching herself off the platform. I followed, realized what I'd done, and screamed.

"Relax!" she said. "Try not to hit anything!"

I screamed louder.

Fortunately the ropes were tied to branches, not tree trunks, so I started to slow halfway through the swing. The Witch reached the next tree, grabbed another rope, and pushed off. I followed with less grace.

"Who takes care of all these ropes?" I yelled.

"Trained monkeys!"

"... Seriously?"

Under the moonlight, we sailed from tree to tree. We swung over the forest floor, sometimes so low our toes brushed the ground. We stepped onto branches, hopped from limb to limb, and ran down bridges of fallen trees. We flew along ziplines, leaped across ravines, and always, sailed from tree to tree.

I don't know how long we did that—moved effortlessly through the forest. I was lost in the moment, and the moment was movement. There was the moonlight, the forest, and the wind. At some point I found the Witch clinging to me (or was I clinging to her?) and we swung together in endless rhythm.

We took the longest possible route, I'm sure.

When we finally broke apart, we had landed in a tree overlooking a clearing. As we adjusted our clothes I couldn't help it—I beat my chest and let loose the victory cry of the bull ape. It ululated across the wilderness and stirred up clouds of birds.

"Why do men always have to make a big deal out of it?" said the Witch, shaking her head.

I grinned and wiped sweat from my brow. "It was great. Did we have to go all this way for that?"

"Not really. I just wanted to make it up to you for the mind-reading trick." She pulled a bow and quiver from a hidden cache.

"Whoa, whoa," I said, stepping back. "I thought we had something special!"

She smiled. "Look to the clearing."

There was a ring of standing stones. Sparks jumped from stone to stone.

"A fairy ring," she said. "My ancestors discovered it. It's a soft spot between realities—and we're about to get a visitor."

"How do you know?"

"I am the Witch of Deepwood. The forest tells me everything."

"So does a tree make a sound when it falls? Does a bear shit in the woods?"

"Shush," said the Witch. "Watch."

The sparks multiplied, arcing among the monoliths like a thing alive. The air smelled of hot copper and my hair stood on end. Energy was building, humming, and I opened my senses to discover their source. Force lines sprang into my Sight and I saw a many-sided whirlpool inside the circle. The entire magic field was turning and churning, preparing for an awesome feat of magic.

Pop.

A spherical area disappeared, instantly replaced by another section of air and dirt—and one more thing. There was a halfling inside the fairy ring. She slumped unconscious in a shiny metal chair.

"Pull her out, Angrod."

"Why me?"

"Because I said so. Hurry or the ring will teleport you both to a dark place."

"Are you sure it won't just return her?"

"Of course. Now go!"

I ran inside the circle. The halfling's chair had wheels and handles and I realized she was a *crippled* halfling. I grasped the handles and pushed her out of there.

Just in time too. We'd just cleared the stones when there was a *pop* and a sudden wind, like a reverse explosion. I shivered. We'd almost been teleported into a vacuum.

"Nice work," the Witch said. "Now let's take a look at our interdimensional refugee."

The halfling girl was strange, to say the least.

There were synthetic materials in her clothes. Quite ordinary for an elf or dwarf, but halflings preferred homespun. Being nonmagical, they only used natural fabrics. These clothes were better than anything halflings could make, and yet they had seams and stitches. The manufacturers had access to artificial fabrics but knew nothing of tailoring spells that shaped material on a molecular level.

The wheeled chair was made of several parts, like a dwarven product, and it too demonstrated great manufacturing skill. It must have been expensive, though it was unnecessary in Brandish, where even the poorest halfling could afford elven healing. The girl was paralyzed, it was true, but repairing spinal cords was only a day's work for a skilled water mage.

Going through her pockets, the Witch found coins and banknotes. I had just begun to examine the foreign money when the girl woke up. She screamed when she saw us. I do not think she had seen an elf before.

The Witch grabbed the girl's head in both hands. She stared deeply into the halfling's eyes, which fluttered as the spell took effect.

"Pleasant dreams," she said, as the girl fell into a deep sleep.

"Tell me about these fairy rings," I said to the Witch.

She sat cross-legged in the grass with the girl on her lap. With my Sight I saw the active spell glyphs. She was writing information directly into the girl's brain, a delicate bit of work, but the elven woman hadn't even broken a sweat. Somehow she drew strength from the forest. Cruix had said that stone could think. Apparently, so could wood.

"This is the only ring left in Brandish. There are others, but they're in the barbarian lands. The teleportation happens every few weeks. Usually it's just a few insects, maybe a bird or field mouse, but sometimes we get a halfling."

"Just halflings?"

"Don't you know? Elves, dwarves, and humans are unique to our world. We evolved from a common ancestor, and our common ancestor came from somewhere else. Halflings come from that place."

"A world of halflings?" I said in disbelief.

"A world without magic. With them as the dominant species."

I sat down. "That… would make sense."

In fact, it confirmed my theories about the origins of humanoid life. We *did* come from elsewhere. The fairy rings were the way. Unfortunately, according to the Witch it was a one-way trip.

The girl shifted in her sleep, then settled down. When she woke she'd speak a little Elvish—about as much as a tourist. She'd also have an abridged guide to Brandish, mostly about things that could kill her if she weren't careful.

"You must get many of these visitors," I told the Witch.

"Every few years. The ring was due for it, which is why I brought you. These people arrive confused and scared. We shelter them a few days and then send them on their way."

"Where do they go?" I wondered. "And what can I do?"

"Most adjust to their new lives and settle down somewhere. Many make their way to the cities, where they try to have normal lives. A few get it in their heads that they're adventurers and get eaten by wyverns."

"They never find each other and band together?"

"It's a big world. Angrod, I'm showing you this because you need to know. I see great things in your future. You will make decisions that will affect not just our people, but also the entire world."

I scratched my head. "People keep telling me that, but as far as I know I'm still going to die in a few weeks. Can we dispense with the riddles? Just give me the plain truth."

The Witch smiled. "Once you can see the source of magic, all will be revealed."

"Where am I?"

It was dawn. We had allowed the girl to awaken.

"You are in Deepwood Forest. I am the mistress of this place, and this is Angrod Veneanar, gentleman adventurer."

"How can I… understand? How can I… speak? Oh, right—magic."

"We will bring you to my village. You can rest there until you're ready to move on. If you'll step this way?"

"Step…?"

"Take my hand."

The girl took the Witch's hand and the elf pulled her to her feet. She gasped, but then her legs steadied. She took a few shaky steps from the wheelchair.

"I… can… walk!" she said, her face lighting up. She took several more steps and grew more confident. "I walk—again!"

She let go of the Witch to walk even further. For a few minutes she enjoyed the use of her legs. Then she frowned. "I'm never… seeing my family again, will I?"

"I'm sorry."

"I'm… grateful. But… shouldn't I… sadder?"

"I dampened your emotions, for a time. The grief will come, but gradually."

"I want to… cry… if you don't mind."

"It's all right," the Witch said, and hugged her.

I looked away as the halfling had a good cry. They did that a lot, but they were stronger than they looked.

Chapter 16

"Why can't I go with you?" Conrad asked.

He watched as we loaded supplies into the little sailboat. He'd wanted to help, but I told him to stay close to Sandy, the halfling from another world.

"I can ride, I can shoot, I won't be a burden at all," he insisted.

"That's true," I said, "but I've already got two sidekicks."

"Hey!" Minos said.

"I thought we were friends," the boy said, his voice breaking. I sighed and turned to him.

"Conrad, little buddy, this is a life-and-death mission. Once we get on that boat we're going to be risking our lives again. You're a tough guy, but it's too dangerous for you. I will not allow it."

"But—"

"Not even if you grow a moustache right this moment."

"A good leader never asks for something he can't do himself," Heronimo said. He had a sack over each shoulder but he set them down to clap the boy on the back. "It's been good to know you, kid, but your mission is to reconnect with your people. You've got that girl to take care of."

"Hmph," Conrad said. "She's useless. Can't ride, can't fight, can't even track."

"She's an orphan just like you."

Minos came over and handed Conrad a small purse. From the way it clinked it carried more than a few gold pieces.

"Travelling money," the little dwarf said. "It's half my stash, so it ought to last you a while. I also give to you our horses and mules—may they serve you well!"

"Thank you, Minos."

The dwarf flushed and turned to Heronimo and me. "Well, and where are all the supplies? Come on, we haven't all day."

Meerwen stood in the middle of the ruined halfling village. Her face grim, she scanned the bodies for clues.

Feanaro, her second-in-command, offered his opinion: "Looks like Angrod picked up a pair of killers."

She looked around to see that no one else was near, then leaned close. "Don't be a fool, Fen. These halflings may have put up a fight, but from the look of their wounds they were already dead."

"Forbidden magic?"

"Forbidden water magic. And Angrod only scored average in that area."

She walked around, tracing the action by the arrangement of the bodies. "It started in this cottage. The human was over six feet tall and massive. He also drew first blood, and the battle spilled onto the street. A savage and undisciplined fighter—the dwarf—killed many here, then duelled the blacksmith. This knot of headless chickens must be where the human was distracted. And these corpses with their heads blown off or caved in, that must have been Angrod."

"So they were ambushed. Who else is hunting the dragon?"

"I don't know." Meerwen frowned. She thought of her father. "But I wonder."

The task force tracked Angrod until they reached the bridge to Deepwood.

"Looks all right," said Feanaro. "Is that a woman?"

Meerwen rode up to the woman, who sat beside the bridge. As the elf drew closer she saw that the woman was crying.

"Good woman, why do you weep? Did you come from the village behind me?"

"I did," the woman said. "My son and I, we survived the massacre. M-my husband died letting us escape." She started weeping again.

"I'm sorry," Meerwen said. She dismounted and offered her handkerchief. "Where is your son now?"

"They took him! An elf, a human, and a d-dirty dwarf! Said they needed someone to look after their mules."

"Those fiends," Feanaro said.

"This makes no sense," Meerwen said, but her lieutenant continued:

"We shall not rest, madam, until we have rescued your baby and brought his kidnappers to justice!" And he galloped down the bridge.

"She didn't say he was a baby—aw hell."

They watched the royal knight thunder down the living bridge. Moments later he was pounding back, eyes wide. "How'd you get here so fast?"

"We never left, dumbass."

"But I just—" and he turned and rode back across the bridge, reappearing minutes later. "Is someone messing with my mind?"

"It wouldn't take much," Meerwen said. She picked up a stick and drew a line in the dirt, then bent the line back until it merged with itself. "They cut off the bridge from the other side, doubled it back, and cast an illusion. We're not getting across that way."

We cast off from Deepwood's western shore and sailed toward the Southern Sea. The plan was to hug the coast, head north, and round the cape at Bone Valley. Ultimately we would make landfall in Corinthe Bay.

The Witch had been prepared to help us on our way, but she hadn't planned to give us her people's best boat. That was where Minos came in. Thanks to his purse we were once again well-equipped, and as Heronimo was a skilled sailor the trip went smoothly.

I'd been lucky with my companions. I wouldn't have gotten as far without the human's skill or the dwarf's generosity. Though this adventure would almost certainly end badly for me, it was an adventure nevertheless.

The trip downstream was uneventful, which was a nice change. If we had travelled overland, we probably would have gotten into all sorts of side missions. The only problem was that the way was boring. There wasn't much to do except drink and play cards.

"Wish we had some women," Heronimo said. "Hit me."

I dealt him another card. "Why would you want that?"

"This boat's a real sausage fest, haven't you noticed?"

"Can't say I have. We're on a quest, not a pleasure cruise."

"Mm," he said, and took another drink from the bottle. Thanks to the Witch there was plenty of mead on board. "It's just been a long boat ride."

"At least there's plenty to drink."

"Yes, but I'm a wine, women, and song kind of man. Say—"

"I will not endure more of your singing."

"You said you liked *Show Me the Way Home*."

"Music is not one of your many talents. Yours is more of a battlefield voice. And don't even think about any traditional songs."

"But Three Battles and Three Funerals is my favourite!"

"Ugh. So depressing. And why are you so horny? Don't tell me you didn't have any opportunities back there. The wood elf babes were practically hanging off you."

He grinned. "They had lots of places to hang from."

I looked at Minos, who was scrutinizing his cards. He had delicate hands, for a dwarf.

"How about you, Angrod?" Heronimo asked. "Did you get any action? Eighteen."

"Depends on what you mean by action. Also, twenty-one."

"Eighteen," Minos said. He showed his cards and I raked in the chips.

"Wish we knew another card game," Heronimo said. "You sure you don't wanna learn Dragon Poker?"

"I have enough dragons in my life, thank you."

"Anyway, something happened between you and the alpha witch. How was she?"

I smiled. "Let's say she was a swinger."

We laughed. I dealt out more cards and we all had a drink.

"I don't remember much but I think I did get lucky," Heronimo said. "She was short, cute, and curvy. Lots of fun!"

I thought I heard someone say *eep*, but that could've been my imagination. It's never entirely silent on a boat.

"But she was gone when I woke up."

I looked at him, I looked at Minos, and I looked a Heronimo again. At the back of my head, Cruix was humming something about strange fancies and a girl in her brother's clothes.

No way.

Yes way.

But he has a beard! A long, luxurious beard, the envy of every smooth-chinned elf.

Search your feelings!

But... the beard.

"Hit me," Minos said.

"I wouldn't hit a lady."

"What?"

"I mean, like candy from a baby."

"Huh?"

Now that I thought about it, it made sense. In the beginning Minos had been so boisterously macho it was like a parody of masculinity. Other details also fell into place: The unusual modesty, the insistence on sleeping apart, and the lingering glances at Heronimo's butt.

Now that I could admit it to myself, there was great deal more sway in Minos's hips than I'd ever seen on a dwarf. And we'd never once pissed together in the unspoiled wilderness.

There wasn't any way to be sure, at least nothing that would allow us to remain friends. I had tried my Sight, but Minos's gear threw up too much static. I'd ask, but that could easily create the awkward situation I was trying to avoid.

We were approaching the marsh. Heronimo proposed a dip. "This will be the last freshwater bath for a while. I don't know about you, but I've never liked bathing in the sea."

So we moored the boat to a tree and stripped down. That is, Heronimo and I got naked and dived in. Minos stayed aboard and tried to look elsewhere.

"Come on, the water's fine!" Heronimo said. "Take off that chain mail and get in here!"

"I prefer sponge baths," Minos said. "Dwarves panic when their faces are submerged, did you know that?"

Quick as a snake, Heronimo grabbed Minos and pulled—the dwarf went headfirst into the water.

"Heronimo!" I said.

"It's okay, the river's shallow here. See? I can totally stand in it."

"Can Minos?"

"... Shit."

He reached down into the murky water, looking for our dwarf friend. "Help me fish him out!"

I waded over and searched for Minos in the murky water.

"Wait, I think I've got him!" Heronimo said. His hand came up with the dwarf's beard—and nothing else. We stared at a dripping mass of hair.

"Oh, gods," Heronimo said. "We drowned his beard!"

Minos burst out of the water. She climbed out of the river, gasping and sputtering. "Heronimo, don't *do* that!"

She saw us holding her beard. "Um."

I say *she*, because without it she was clearly a woman.

"A false beard?" Heronimo said. "Is't possible?"

"Give me that," I said. I brushed the hairs over my chin and they stuck fast. They changed colour too, going from brown to curly black, just like my head hair. I was suddenly in possession of a gorgeous moustache and beard. "Hah! Finally!"

Heronimo stared at Minos. "You're a girl?"

"Yes!" Minos said. She tore an amulet from her neck and her voice lost its booming quality. "Yes, I am a woman!"

"I've heard that voice before!"

"I am Beardman!" I said. There were still quite a few magic hairs in my hand, so I brushed them under Heronimo's chin, where they turned a glorious blonde. "Behold my sidekick Neckbeard! We fight crime."

"I've seen those lips before."

"You are refusing to be distracted," I said. "Okay, Minos is a girl. Naturally we'll want to hear her story, but really, is it such a big deal?"

"It's Mina, actually. Mina Minasdottir."

"Holy hell, that was you?" Heronimo said.

"I was drunk!"

"Wait, *you're* Short, Cute, and Curvy?"

"Holy balls," Heronimo said. "I feel so, so violated."

Mina crossed her arms and turned bright pink. "That's not how you felt that night."

Heronimo was so shocked he couldn't close his mouth. I patted him on the shoulder. "It looks like you got your wish, my trusty sidekick. This quest is now co-educational."

"I just wanted to go on adventures," she said.

We sat around the dining table in our bathrobes. Mina had finally taken off her helmet and her hair flowed down her shoulders in an auburn wave.

She looked very different out of her armour. Her mail shirt had been more padded than we thought. She was still well-padded, but differently.

Dwarves are short and stocky, but it turns out the women aren't nearly as heavy. Mina could probably pick up Heronimo if she wanted to, but it was also easy to picture her in a ball gown.

"So you're not a dwarven prince, but a dwarven princess?" I asked.

"That is correct," she said. "My da is Magnus Wolfsson, chieftain of the Ironore Mountains."

"Wait, your father is named Big Man, Son of Wolf? That is a badass name."

"Most definitely badass," Heronimo said.

We had a moment of silence to reflect on how badass it was.

"Anyway, what made you decide to go adventuring in disguise?"

She shrugged. "I didn't just leave the Ironore Mountains. I *escaped*. All my life I've wanted to be a warrior and have my exploits sung throughout the land, but there's never been a woman adventurer among the dwarves. When they said they were sending me to Drystone to meet next elf king, I decided I'd had enough."

"Um," I said.

"You disguised yourself so your father wouldn't find you?" Heronimo asked. "You were not trying to trick us?"

"I swear, I never meant to hurt you two. You were my best friends, and I treasure how you treated me like one of the boys. Well, you thought I *was* one of the boys."

"Is that why all the magical equipment?" I asked.

"I stole them from my da's personal guard. There were four of them and I took their most precious artefacts."

"And what would those artefacts be?"

She pointed at her scattered panoply. "The Boots of Speed. The Belt of Strength. The Mail Shirt of Protection. The Helm of Anti-Concussion."

"Is it me, or are dwarves bad at naming things? You make lovely stuff, but never call them anything cool."

"Shut up. You understood instantly, didn't you?"

She raised the mail shirt, which was as light and as fine as lace. "I can barely feel it on my shoulders but it's proof against nearly anything. When struck, the links become impenetrably hard. *This* helmet encloses my head in a cushion of force so my brain cannot bounce against my skull."

"Very useful," I said, "but they could be improved by more creative names. Why not *the Helm of Stone Head* or *the Mail Shirt of Dragon Skin?*"

"First, because dragon skin isn't actually impenetrable," Mina said. "And second, would *you* buy a Helm of Stone Head? For all you might know it might turn your brain to stone."

"That would be redundant for you, Angrod." Heronimo said.

"Good one!" I said. We high-fived.

"There's also the Buckler of Blocking, the Axe of Crazy, and the Crossbow of Intuition. The buckler always defends against attack, the axe fills the wielder with rage, and the crossbow only shoots at the best possible moment."

"You use these trinkets to multiply what little skill you have." Heronimo said.

She stuck out her tongue. "I always wanted to learn weapons, but dwarven princesses aren't allowed. I also have the Ring of Slow Time, the Ring of Regeneration, the Amulet of Gender Flip, and the Beard of Fakery."

"The Amulet of Gender Flip? You mean—"

"It makes women seem more masculine and men more feminine."

I snatched it from the table and put it on. Heronimo and Mina stared.

"Oh, my," Mina said.

"That isn't right," Heronimo said.

"I don't feel any different?"

"Angrod, I'm not a lesbian but even I am tempted."

"You totally have boobs."

"What?" I tore off the amulet. I looked at Heronimo and started toward him. He leaped out of his seat and tore out of the cabin. There was a splash.

I looked at the thing in my hand. "Why would one of your father's personal guards need this?"

"They're more of a personal hit squad."

"And you stole their stuff, and also the treasury?"

"What treasury? That was just my allowance."

Chapter 17

he rest of the trip was uneventful. Heronimo and Mina weren't speaking to each other, which is just as well. While there was just enough room in the boat for three people, there wasn't any for one couple and one bachelor.

We hugged the coast right up to the cape, at which point Heronimo took us further out to sea.

"The winds around a cape are treacherous," he said from the helm. "Best to head for deeper water."

"I don't know if that's such a good idea. We're roughly between the mainland and Luxylgard, which is pretty remote."

Mina was looking at the map. "Luxylgard doesn't look very far away."

"These waters are especially deep. The map doesn't show it, but there's a trench between the cape and the island. What does it say on the map? It says *Here be eldritch things*."

"What's *eldritch?*" Heronimo asked.

"Slimy, I think," I said.

"Well, if anything slimy comes over the side, I will hit it with my sword."

A great gaping shark landed on the deck. It was surprisingly small, but that's because it was missing half its body.

"You're gonna need a bigger sword," I said.

Something hit us. The entire boat shook. A dark shape swam past.

"We're under attack!" Mina said. BOOM. Another impact. I steadied myself on deck. "Quick! Get below! Full power to the engines!"

Mina hurried into the cabin, then popped out. "We don't *have* engines!"

"Do something!" Heronimo said.

TEETH burst out of the water. They were attached to one huge reptile.

"Sea wyvern!" I said.

It was huge—nearly fifty feet—and armoured in blue-green scales. It was stockier than its land cousin and its wings were made for swimming. It wasn't any brighter though, so it started chewing on the boat.

Heronimo drew his sword and stabbed at its snout, but it was like a pin to a pit bull. Mina ran up with her crossbow but the beast was shaking its head so hard she couldn't get a shot.

"We're taking water!" she said.

"It's trying to roll!" Heronimo said. The boat was disintegrating in the wyvern's jaws. The deck tilted and he slid into its mouth.

"Heronimooo!" Mina said, but then the human tumbled out. His sword was bloody. "I got its tongue," he said.

The ship continued to sink. We were wading now.

"Grab our stuff," I told my friends. "Heronimo, Mina. Clear the deck. I'm about to do... something."

I remembered that wyverns were only afraid on one thing. It didn't seem useful, because how often do you have one of those lying around? "Get ready to tread water!" I said.

"We're ready," Mina said. "Do it."

"This is going to hurt," I said, and walked toward the wyvern. My shirt collar tore and the buttons flew free. I kicked off my shoes and my talons dug into the deck. My shirt stretched over my shoulders and I tore it away with my teeth. The boat sank under my weight. There was pain, yes, but I accepted it. It washed over me and gave fuel to my rage.

I was a dragon again. I'd traded days of my life for Cruix's power. I stuck my face in the sea wyvern's snout and roared.

"GET THE *FUCK* OUTTA MY FACE!"

I swear the wyvern turned pale. It paddled backward, swamping Heronimo and Mina. They clung to the wreckage, the weight of their gear dragging them down. I grabbed my floundering friends and vaulted out of the sea. My wings caught the wind and we flew toward dry land.

"Angrod!" Mina said. "Can you not hold onto Heronimo so tightly? I've got my armour on, but your claws are digging into him!"

"You okay, man? I loosen my grip I'll drop you. There are other things in the water!"

"S'fine, I'm okay! You didn't pierce anything vital!"

"Save me from macho bullshit," Mina said.

We flew over the cape. We were gliding over Bone Valley when we saw them.

Oh no, Cruix said.

"Gods!" Mina said.

They didn't call it Bone Valley because it was a desert. It was, yes, but it was also a dragon graveyard.

Death was everywhere. It was like looking down from a high place and seeing a city stretched beneath you, except the streets were paved with skulls and the houses were made of ribs. So many bones that the desert couldn't bury them. They rose from the sand, sharp and white.

Many of the dragon skeletons were intact. They did not sprawl across the dunes, but curled on their sides, arms and legs drawn up to their bodies. Massive by humanoid standards, they seemed fragile and small and not at all fearsome.

"My people," I said. "My people."

"Angrod?" Mina said. "We're losing height!"

"My people!"

A mother and her hatchling lay huddled together in death. The larger dragon had draped its wings over the smaller. The little one's head was tucked into the curve of its mother's neck.

"Here we go!" Mina said.

I didn't know if I was dragon or elf anymore. I forgot to fly. The desert leaped to meet me—

"Angrod? Angrod?"

I was walking in the graveyard, the wrecks of ancient dragons all around me. I was an elf again, and naked, and going in circles.

"Angrod?" Mina said.

"I see all my people, stretching back to the beginning of dragonkind. I see my mother's mother and her mother's mother. I see friends and former friends. I see flight mates and nest mates."

"Angrod, something's wrong with Heronimo."

I pointed. "Look there—those are my grandmother's bones. I'd know those horns anywhere. And there, the bones of my sister."

"Angrod, he's badly wounded."

"… and that one would be Chad, I always hated him…"

"He's not healing!"

For ages we stumbled in the desert of despair, tears dripping down my chin.

"I have counted the skulls and found not one missing," I said. "These bleached things are all the remains of my people. Oh, my people, would that I had joined you! I am the last, the last."

"Heronimo is dying!"

"I don't care. I don't care. What is death next to extinction? What is one individual life weighed against the light of an entire species?"

"Good question!"

I stopped. Blinked. It was a very deep voice.

The capran rode up. His horns were oiled and shiny. His build and his armour said he was a fighting man. His aura of crackling power said he was a mage. He was wizard and warrior both.

"I am Arawn, king of the caprans!"

I shook my head. "Why can I never meet normal people, o king?"

He laughed. "Heroes never just meet people. Not when they're on a quest."

"Do I look like a hero?"

He leaned forward. "You have the look of someone on a quest. Therefore, you must be a hero. And heroes only meet two kinds of people: Allies or enemies."

"Good sir, can you help our friend?" Mina said.

"We shall see."

"This is bad," Arawn said

Heronimo lay in a makeshift bed, his wounds hastily bandaged. He twisted and moaned, lost in delirium. The stains in his bandages were growing.

"The sea wyvern's bite carries one of the strongest venoms in the world. It's a wonder this man is still alive. He seems to be fighting the poison—but there is no antidote. He shall soon die."

Mina wailed and buried her face in my shoulder. I turned to the king. "Can you do something?"

Arawn nodded. "We can rebuild him. We have the sorcery. All is not lost, young hero."

"Name your price," Mina said. "My father is chieftain of Ironore and he can supply you with this human's weight in gold."

"I do not deal in gold, but in favours," said Arawn, looking at me. "And this day I will only deal with you, elf who would be king."

"How—"

"We must stabilize your friend. Stand back and I will slow his metabolism."

When he said, "Stand back," Mina and I stepped several yards back. Capran magic is unpredictable. It's easily as powerful as elven magic, but nowhere as precise. You know Pithe Lake? A capran did that. He was trying to dig a well.

Arawn gestured with his left hand and the ground shuddered. Dust rose in a perfect circle, and when it cleared Heronimo was no longer breathing.

Mina drew her axe but I held her back. "His aura's still flickering. He's alive, and in perfect hibernation!"

Birth

I woke up. I had never opened my eyes before. After so many months spent becoming, after so much time spent preparing, it was the day. My world had grown too small for me, and my limbs ached against their confinement. It was time.

Slowly, slowly, I used my egg tooth to chip at the leathery walls. Eventually, I broke through. Air rushed in and I rested from my labours. I chirped—how small I sounded! I could hear my mother digging for me, removing the hot, reeking vegetation mounded over my egg.

I broke the last of the shell and tumbled into the world, a wet scrap of flesh. My mother crooned and covered me with a wing. Finally, the world had an up and a down. It had air, and light and presumably, food. Anxious to catch my first meal, I tested all six limbs. I stretched my legs, flexed my claws, and flapped wings too small to fly.

I was alive. I was born.

I looked up at my mother and saw a fleshless skull.

"Aauugh!" I said.

"Bad dreams, elf?" Arawn asked.

"Someone else's, actually."

"Those are the worst," said the king of the goat people. He rolled out of his sleeping bag, abundantly naked, and ambled over to a nearby ribcage for the first piss of the day.

"Aaaahh," he said. "That's good. Nothing like small beer to ensure an early morning." He scratched a farted. He saw my expression and laughed. "Those are a king's farts, my little elf, and I decree they smell like roses!"

"Ugh," Mina said. "Why does it stink of a barn?" She sat up and saw Arawn. "Eep!"

"Haha! Wake up, princess! Time for breakfast!"

I looked at the capran. His rough, handsome face sported a goatee (of course) and he was nearly as tall and as muscular as Heronimo, but much hairier. He became positively shaggy past the knees. His feet ended in cloven hooves. As he approached he smelled strongly of sweat and musk. The odour was just slightly gamy.

I looked at Heronimo. He was still tied to the travois we'd meant to attach to Arawn's horse. His vital signs were as low as they could be, short of turning him to stone.

We breakfasted quickly and struck camp. Arawn said, "To me, my armour!" and the pieces arranged themselves around him. The angular plates settled smoothly on his body, the breastplate melding with the backplate, the vambraces and rerebraces snapping onto his arms. The greaves wrapped around his legs and the pauldrons settled on his shoulders. Smaller metal pieces swirled around him, forming chain mail in places and armouring his hands as he flexed them. In less than a second he was fully and fearsomely protected.

"Remarkable," I said.

"Nothing but the finest dwarven craftsmanship," he said. His visor was much more goatlike than his actual face. "We considered making it ourselves, but blew up a castle wing."

"It must have cost you a fortune," Mina said.

"Accidents happen in the lab all the time. The suit did cost a pretty pile, though. Shall we go?"

"Lead on," I said.

"Tanngrisnir, to me!" he said, and his black warhorse trotted up. Arawn vaulted into the saddle and the horse took off.

"What about Heronimo?!" Mina said. She snatched up the makeshift sled and tried to run after Arawn, but the goat-king swung around and started to circle. Dust rose. Arawn completed his orbit once... twice... three times. He gestured, and the world dropped from under us.

We were in a different valley when the air cleared. The sun and the mountains were in the same places, but everything was green, green, *green*. Arawn laughed. "Welcome to the Silver World!"

Chapter 18

The caprans don't call it the Silver World, of course, the same way we didn't call Brandish *The Iron World* like the caprans did. I had asked Arawn about the names and he said, "I can't really say."

The king's retinue had waited for him in the valley, which in this world was grassland. I had never encountered capran warriors before, so the sight of three hundred soldiers was a bit of a shock. I almost went full dragon before I saw that they were simply standing around.

An officer rode up. "Welcome back, your majesty."

"Thank you, Grahothy. We must return to the capital at once!"

Fine capran horses were provided and soon we were cantering out of the valley.

"That went smoothly," I told Arawn. "Do you visit Bone Valley often?"

"I go there to meditate," he said. "But sometimes I visit your world to meet women—don't look at me like that! They come of their own free will and they can leave anytime. We're not centaurs."

"Centaurs!" Mina said. "So they exist?"

"They did," Arawn said. He patted his mount. "Tanngrisnir is part-centaur, which is why he's so smart and strong. The half-horses created us caprans as well. We are their final legacy."

I leaned forward in the saddle. "So it's true, your people are a product of crossbreeding?"

"We prefer to call it uplifting," he said with dignity.

The Silver World was much like my own. The vegetation was somewhat different and the mountains seemed taller, but otherwise the worlds were identical. I was the first elf to set foot in the capran homeland, but I was jaded after everything that had happened. How many experiences of a lifetime can you have?

I glanced behind to check on Heronimo's litter. The travois now hung between two horses. The rider on the lead horse gave me a wave.

Arawn's bodyguard was well-equipped. The light cavalry was dressed in silk and leather and carried bows. The heavy cavalry was dressed in silk and mail and carried lances. Everyone had a scimitar and round shield. They laughed among themselves, but rode in perfect formation, their horses almost in lockstep.

Mina sidled up to me and we dropped behind Arawn. "Have you ever seen capran warriors?" she asked.

I shook my head. "I've only met traders and tourists. I've never considered that caprans might even *have* an army."

A startled pheasant took wing and was pierced by an arrow. A soldier rode up and plucked it from the ground. A hare bounded off but was impaled upon a lance.

"And here we thought they were just party animals," I said.

The riders snapped up game throughout the day. They even dressed the meat from the saddle. They continued to talk and joke even as they hunted. We lost not a second's worth of travel.

We changed horses frequently, each man having two or three extra animals. Our mounts were so well-trained it was possible to sleep in the saddle at full trot. A day and a night thus passed. I awoke as we approached a familiar city.

It was smaller than I remembered, and the architecture was different, but there was no mistaking its location within sight of Pithe Mountain and the Northern Sea. I turned to Arawn.

"Corinthe?" I asked.

"Zith'ra."

We watched the priestesses make their preparations. Covered in tattoos, they painted similar symbols all over Heronimo's flesh.

"What are those things?" Mina asked.

"Part numbers," Arawn said. "So there's no confusion when they reassemble him."

She looked at me. "Is he serious?"

Arawn continued: "Each sorceress carries a mana stone of unusual size and clarity. Through this stone, she will focus on one of the body's four tissues—epithelial tissue, connective tissue, muscle tissue, or nervous tissue. She will teleport this material into the astral plane and rid it of defects and disease. All four women will then reconstitute the body and awaken it to restored health. At least, that's the idea. In practice, there's always the risk of transcription error."

"What do you mean, *transcription error?*"

"Imagine reading an entire library, then writing it down from memory. Could you do it without making a mistake? That's why it takes four people—they correct each other."

"I have a bad feeling about this," Mina said. "Why are we over here?"

Here was a bunker on the beach, a long way from the ceremonial site, actually a raft out to sea. We watched the ceremony through telescopes.

Arawn admitted there was a chance that a tiny fraction of Heronimo would convert to energy, causing a massive explosion. Mina had to go to a corner and sit down.

I was about to ask another question, but the ritual began. The sorceress with the green tattoos took the northernmost position. She began to speak. Arawn repeated the words for our benefit:

"I, Priestess of Earth, do accept this man's bones. I take them into myself, where they may be strengthened."

The sorceress with the red tattoos took the southernmost station. "I, Priestess of Fire, do accept this man's heart. I take it into myself, that it may be strengthened."

The sorceress with the blue tattoos went to the east, and the one with the orange tattoos went to the west. The Priestesses of Air and Water accepted Heronimo's brain and skin. As we watched, his body disappeared in layers. His flesh turned transparent. His bones turned to glass. He was a living anatomy chart for a moment, and then he vanished. In each woman's hand, a crystal blazed like the sun.

The four sorceresses sat cross-legged on the raft. Their faces still, they stared into the facets of their mana stones.

"They have put their minds into the crystals. Now, we wait."

The ritual could easily take all night, Arawn said. Having converted Heronimo into information, the women were going over every single bit, correcting and improving as they went.

"Wouldn't that take really long?" I asked. We sat in the bunker and drank tea to stay awake.

"Not for us," he said. "We have a special relationship with time. For us, a minute can last a million years."

"What do you do with all that time?"

"Mostly we don't. A taste of eternity can drive one insane. Those sorceresses are going to wipe it from their minds at the end of the ritual."

"That's not so bad."

"Angrod, when purging a million years from your memory, it's all too easy to lose an extra decade. Those women are going to wake up with gaps. Sometimes they forget how to walk or talk."

Mina almost dropped her mug. "That's horrible!"

Arawn shrugged. "I pay them well. And backups were made. They're more like summaries than actual memories, but they do help with the recovery process."

"It's still an awful lot to sacrifice," I said. "What kind of favour is that worth?"

He grinned. "I won't ask you to do anything that goes against your moral code. It will be something you can do, difficult though it may be. It will be a one-time deed of similar value."

"That sounds fair."

"It is very fair. It is good that I am a king and not a shopkeeper."

We looked out to sea where the ritual continued. The women were motionless even as the raft bobbed on the waves.

"They should be halfway done," Arawn said. He looked at me. "As it happens, I know what you can do for me. Someday—and that day may never come—I will call upon you for a year of service. Complete that year and your debt shall be paid, whether or not you survive."

Gulp. "That is acceptable."

"Wait, what do you mean *improving as they go?*" Mina asked. "Is it still going to be Heronimo when they put him back together?"

"Almost certainly," Arawn said. "Same memories, same personality, same species. It's just that the priestesses can't help but make embellishments. They're not machines. This is as much a creative ritual as it is a magical one."

Waiting is hungry work. Fortunately, Arawn had done this before, and there was game pie and venison stew.

I bit into the pie and tasted hare and pheasant. "It's really good. Is this—?"

"It's not from today's hunting, unfortunately. The cook said a proper meat pastry takes longer."

Mina had a spoonful of stew and her eyes grew wide. "A halfling made this!"

I took a taste and had to agree. "I didn't know there were halflings in the Silver World."

"What was the clue?" asked the king. "Was it the spices? The stock?"

"I don't know," she said. "There's just something about halfling cooking. Even the simple dishes fill you up."

"Sticks to your ribs." I said. "Nothing magical about it, but it's pretty amazing."

We busied ourselves with the meal and it was many long minutes before we could speak again. I pushed aside my bowl and accepted a cut cigar from Arawn. Mina declined.

I snapped my fingers and the king and I lit our cigars on the resulting flame.

"Something to drink?" he said, and poured glasses for Mina and me.

"Looks like milk," I said.

"It was. *Kumis* is mare's milk, fermented and freeze-distilled."

"That's where they take out the ice crystals," I explained to Mina. "Makes for a stronger drink."

We both took a sip.

"Wow," she said. "I've never tasted anything like it. It's like… buttermilk and beer?"

"Yoghurt and champagne? It's got a kick, it's pleasantly tart, and it's refreshing."

"Try your cigar," Arawn said.

I took a puff. "Hey now." I took a sip. "That's smooth. Mina, you're missing out."

She crossed her arms. "I never learned to like tobacco. Underground tunnels and secondhand smoke don't mix."

"It's not all tobacco," Arawn said.

"Yeah, haha, I can tell."

We took slow puffs and small sips. We got mellow.

"So do halflings arrive naturally, or do they cross over from our world?"

"There is some immigration from the Iron World," Arawn said. "Halflings bring much-needed skills and talents. They're very welcome in my lands."

"Hard to imagine halflings being welcome anywhere," I said. "I've nothing against them, but they always seem to get the worst of it back home."

"That's elves for you," Mina said, taking a drink. "Not the most accepting." And she flashed me a look.

"What did I ever do to you?" I asked.

"Don't you remember our first meeting? When you *lied* to me?" And she told Arawn what happened.

"I thought we were done with this," I said. "I made something up because I thought it was for the best."

"You didn't trust me. You trusted Heronimo but not me!"

"That was different. We'd almost killed each other."

"And that made you instant friends?"

Arawn cleared his throat. "Combat is a very intimate thing, don't you know. And I maybe you didn't seem very trustworthy because you were masquerading as a man."

"I… I… *Men.*" Mina said. She stood up. "I'm going for a walk."

I finished my drink and put it down. Arawn refilled both our glasses. "That one isn't used to losing," he said. "I stepped in because you were about make things worse by making those same arguments."

"Thanks," I said, raising my glass. "I'm glad I'm not her boyfriend."

"I don't know about that," he said. He took a long drink. "She's short, cute, and curvy. Must be lots of fun."

I admit, I dozed during the night. So did Mina. Only Arawn did not sleep. Instead he just sat there. He said he was experiencing visions.

It was dawn when we saw some activity. The priestesses had opened their eyes. In the centre of the raft, swirling light. Shapes capered and leaped, bouncing off one another like a riot of ghosts.

"I can't see—" Mina said, and then we were blinded. Lightning had struck the raft.

BOOM

"Don't look directly!" Arawn said. "They're bleeding off energy!"

BOOM

"Heronimo!"

BOOM

Then he was on the raft again. He crouched as sparks rolled off his back. He rose and every hair on the back of my neck stood up. His eyes were glowing red.

"Heronimo!" Mina said. "Oh gods, Heronimo!" She burst from the bunker and ran for the surf.

"So how do you feel?" I asked him.

"Good. Strong. Better than ever, and that's honest truth."

"Anything different?" Mina asked. I reached into a pitcher, pulled the water out like so much taffy, and stretched it into a mirror.

Heronimo looked at his reflection. "I don't remember that gap between my teeth being quite so big. And... did someone put my skin on wrong?"

He still had his scars, but they were reversed. A gash that had been on his right shoulder was now on his left. A cut in his left side was now on his right. He was like a mirror image of his old self.

"I don't see anything wrong with your aura," I said. "We should be grateful nothing else is changed."

"Is that a heart-shaped scar on your right buttock?" Mina said.

"I did say they might make embellishments," Arawn said. "At least they didn't leave their signature on your forehead."

Chapter 19

It was raining hard against Meerwen's tent. She sat inside the canvas dome, a lantern giving just enough light to update her journal. She was recording the events of the day. Unlike the official log, nothing written here would be duplicated elsewhere. She could be as truthful as she liked and nobody would know.

Day 37. Another day's hard riding, and little to show for it, apart from the miles covered. That and the attendant aches and blisters. Even I, with my stone-skin training, have had to resort to bag balm. Drat that Angrod. To think that I liked him.

She paused. She'd already ranted about Angrod in previous entries. She didn't feel like wasting any more ink on him. She toyed with her fountain pen, then resumed writing.

Nothing much of consequence has happened since losing his gang at Deepwood. With the bridge out, we had no choice but to cross further downstream and avoid the island entirely. The halfling woman, Grimalda, asked us where Angrod could be going. I was forced to conclude he must be headed for Corinthe, his home city. Thus we found ourselves crossing the Black Plains.

She stopped writing to stare into space. It wasn't true that nothing had happened. Something had happened, she had the wounds to prove it.

On the third day in that damnable desert, human bandits attacked us. They numbered some three dozen horsemen against my sixteen.

She remembered how they came thundering over the rise. They were a crew of rabble, dressed as they were in their mismatched armour. Humans had never been noted for their blacksmithing. Their gear was stolen or scavenged more often than not. The weapons they held high were from wildly different sources—but they all looked deadly. They'd waited until the last second to reveal themselves. Meerwen had just one option:

"Charge!"

Combat mages and royal guardsmen galloped to meet the savages. The air crackled as the mages hurled fireballs and lightning. They hammered several humans out of the saddle but the bandits were soon running for their horses. Damn, but they were resilient. The barbarians were in a ragged formation, the elves in a wedge with Meerwen at its point.

"For Drystone!" she yelled. The barbarians answered with a wordless roar. They met. Steel clashed against steel. Bones crunched. Horses screamed.

A huge bandit swung a saw-toothed sword at her neck but she ducked and plucked his leg from the stirrup, pulling him from his horse. Another bandit came at her with a lance. She knocked it aside, grabbed his right shoulder with her left hand, and yanked him out of the saddle. The unhorsed humans screamed as the elves rode over them.

Three elves had fallen in the initial shock. Twice as many humans were out of action. The fighting turned into a brawl and the dust grew thick in the melee.

A bandit grabbed Meerwen by the collar, but she chopped down on his arm, trapped it, and unhorsed him. He landed on his feet but her horse kicked him in the head. She reached for another bandit and got him in a headlock, also unhorsing him. There were so many bucking and screaming horses, their hooves flailing in every direction. To be afoot was to die.

She leaned aside as a mage shot a fireball past her, then rode alongside a bandit. She reached around, grabbed him by the chin, and broke his neck.

Two more elves had fallen but the humans were down to half. Her knights were some of the best swordsmen in the realm, more than a match for the raiders. One after another, the barbarians fell to elven blades.

"Hack them down!" Meerwen said. *"Hack them down!"*

The bandit chief rode up. He was huge, even for a human, and he rode a gigantic red horse. He also wore a red crested helmet and banner, as if his role wasn't clear enough.

"Stand aside, everyone!" he roared. "This one's mine!"

He spurred his horse forward. They butted, red charger meeting black. They snorted and they circled. The chief had thrown down his hammer to grapple with her. For long minutes they wrestled for advantage. Both had dropped their bridles to grab at each other. Twice Meerwen had to chop down on his arm and thwart an attack. His horse tried to bite her and she elbowed it in the eye. "Stay out of this!"

They fought in a circle. The others kept their distance. The seven surviving elves stood in a ring with a dozen bandits. They watched as their leaders stood in their stirrups and wrestled on horseback.

Finally Meerwen got a hold on his belt. With a grunt of effort, she pulled him from his seat. The elves cheered.

This was no game, though. The chief snarled and smacked his fist into his hand, still ready to fight. Meerwen raised an eyebrow and slid out of the saddle. "You humans don't know when to quit, do you?"

At this point in her recollection she paused and looked at her left arm in its sling. She'd won the fight, of course, but it had cost her. The healer had never seen a hand so thoroughly broken. *Shattered* was the word he'd used. The daily sessions with him were helping, but it would be a while before she could use it. Water magic wasn't good with bone.

While she considered herself a more than competent fighter, she was still more of a generalist than a specialist. She was proficient in all forms of combat and had no glaring weaknesses but she had yet to master unarmed combat, her chosen specialty.

She considered the various classifications among the martial arts. Elves saw every melee weapon as either one-handed, two-handed, or paired. There were three of each kind, hence the Nine Weapons. The Fighting Nuns had a more pacifistic view, and while they did teach weapons they focused on unarmed combat, which they divided into striking and grappling.

There were finer divisions. Students first learned to deliver blows with their hands, then with their feet, and finally with their knees and elbows. They were then taught stand-up grappling, takedowns, and ground fighting. Once they'd grasped those basics, they learned to combine striking with grappling. After that they practiced fighting in teams and against multiple opponents.

Both elven and human arts were taught using a spiral curriculum. The course was repeated several times, each time at a higher level. It was like climbing a spiral staircase. The first time around a beginner became a novice who knew just enough to recognize when they were outclassed. The second time around a novice became a journeyman skilled enough to be a city guardsman or lay nun.

The third time around a student did more of the same, or else taught others. Not everyone could teach but it was by far the better way to gain understanding. Meerwen had been an assistant teacher. Finally, a journeyman would choose a single weapon or style and practice exclusively. Only after they had tested it against all others could they call themselves masters.

Meerwen was not yet a master, but the bandit chief had been. He specialized in *punching*.

The armoured fist crashed into her jaw and Meerwen knew she was in trouble. The human was more than twice her size but just as fast. She saw stars.

"Hah ha haaa!" he said. "Too easy!"

She raised her guard and swung a kick at his knee. He had strong legs and recovered. He went into a crouch and started punching non-stop, a flurry of powerful blows from which she could only retreat His gauntlets were obviously padded. The flanges on the knuckles made them deadly weapons. She slapped away blows that would have killed an ox. Her own gloves were lined with dwarven mail.

She ducked a right hook that would've turned her head to jelly. She slipped a left uppercut that might've pulped her guts. She went for a side kick to the chest but he covered up. She tried to sweep his legs but he crouched and punched low.

They circled, throwing up sand with their feet. Their followers had sorted themselves so one part of the circle was elves and the other part humans. They watched their leaders duel. They also gambled.

"Place your bets, place your bets," said Grimalda. "Who wins and who dies, gents? *Who wins and who dies!*"

The circle buzzed. Money changed hands. Even the wounded sat up and dug into their pockets. Grimalda accepted wagers and handed out tickets.

The bandit chief charged, fists going like pistons. Meerwen slipped and parried but she wasn't too busy to see what was happening. Even Feanaro waved a roll of cash.

"You're making *bets?*" she yelled.

"She's giving good odds! I bet on you to win!"

"Not to kill him?"

"The odds aren't *that* good."

"I'm not through with you yet!" the chief said. Meerwen had barely covered her ribs before an uppercut slammed into them. She gasped. He followed with another uppercut, then a hook to the jaw. The world exploded and she found herself on the ground.

"Get up, you wimp!" he said.

"I don't think so," she said, and kicked where she lay. She caught him on the shin and he bellowed. She pressed him with more kicks, then scissored his front leg and took him down. He fell on his hands and she sprang up and punched him in the kidneys.

"Aaargh!" he said, hitting the dirt. He rolled, but it gave her time to find her feet.

"Take me for an amateur?" she said. "You'll pay for that mistake!"

"I'll kill you! My fists will have your blood on them!"

He attacked, but anger had taken his skill and she landed more blows than he did. However, his strength was easily a match for her own magically-enhanced power and he brushed aside her punches and kicks. When she managed to land a right cross he merely grunted.

"Not bad. Gimme some gold and I might let you walk away!"

"You can't escape!" she said.

The fight continued. The people watching were silent and tense. Meerwen's head still ached from the man's first punch and it looked like he had limitless stamina. She had to end this quickly.

She lowered her guard to tempt him and he responded with a straight punch. She chopped it aside with her left hand, then grabbed his wrist with the same hand and *squeezed.*

She drew all of the local magic, imagining it rising up from under her feet. Pain flashed in her arm but she brushed it aside and focused on pushing the limits of her strength. She was a machine, and not the gentle kind.

The man screamed. It was like being caught in a vise. The steel gauntlet crumpled under her fingers and still she squeezed. Flesh pulped, bone shattered, and still she squeezed. Desperate, he jerked his other hand back and punched with all his might.

"KIA!" she said, intercepting his fist with her own.

"Aaugh!" he said. His left gauntlet flew apart. The impact threw pieces everywhere and what was left was warped and useless. The hand inside was badly crushed. So was Meerwen's, but the chain mail concealed this by turning rigid. She let go the other man's hand and the bandit chief fell to his knees. "My hands! My beautiful hands!"

"How's it feel, getting beaten up by a tiny girl?" she said. She looked around at the circle and saw fear in everyone's face. "Enough! My men and I hold the advantage. We could arrest you, but we are on a mission. Leave before I call a royal patrol."

"As for you," she said to their fallen leader, "go back to your wife and kids!"

The human bandits gathered their wounded before retreating. They headed seaward, where longships no doubt awaited.

Meerwen stood with her hands on her hips, a sneer on her face. She watched them leave. When they had disappeared she turned to her second-in-command. "Feanaro? You're in charge for now."

Then she toppled backward and landed unconscious in the sand.

When she woke up, she was at an inn. Feanaro had gotten her the best room.

"Are we still in the desert?" she asked.

"On the outskirts," he said, holding a bowl and a spoon. "Eat something, you'll feel better."

She waved the spoon away. "Report first. Casualties?"

"We're down three men: Marcanon, Balanidren, and Eruinon. Except for you, everyone else got away with light wounds." He pointed at her right hand. "The other was easy enough to mend—just torn muscles and tendons—but your right hand was pulped. The glove had gone completely rigid and we had to undo the enchantment to slip it off."

"I suppose the men are ashamed that their leader fainted."

"Actually, they were impressed that you lasted as long. That was quite the biggest human we'd ever seen. And you won! I could live on my winnings for a year."

"I'm glad the experience has enriched you."

The innkeeper knocked. "Just checking on our hero. You and your men can stay for free, courtesy of the townspeople." The halfling smiled. "Those bandits had been preying on our town for months. You dealt with them decisively!"

"This is a halfling settlement, I take it?"

"Oh yes. We were defenceless against the marauders. Things had gotten so bad we sent people to the Ironore Mountains."

"To hire a few swordsmen?"

"No, to buy guns."

Chapter 20

Meerwen lowered her pen and considered what she'd written. They'd spent two days recuperating in town, spending the money they'd won. Halflings were good at entertaining.

"When you don't have magic, you have to reach for every advantage you can get," the innkeeper explained.

They left the town poorer in cash and richer in experience. They'd also left Grimalda behind. The woman had wanted to be there for her son, but Meerwen insisted she stay with her own kind.

The elf had been suspicious. Grimalda was a good rider, even for a farm girl. She'd also fought the bandits —plucking Feanaro's sword from its scabbard and charging into battle with an eager yell. She'd cut down three barbarians and was hacking at a fourth when Meerwen engaged the bandit chief.

Grimalda was also built more like a human. She massed about as much as a male elf and her shapeless dress wasn't enough to conceal a mighty figure. Meerwen didn't know what she was up to, but wanted none of it.

"That halfling stays here," Meerwen told Feanaro. "Be sure she doesn't follow."

"Are you certain? We've gotten close, she and I, and she's really worried about her son."

"Are you letting personal feelings cloud your judgment?"

The young knight looked at the floor and blushed. "She's just being friendly."

"I don't trust her. Tell her we'll send word as soon as we've rescued her son. That's an order, Fen. That woman is dangerous."

Thunder boomed. It was still raining but the tent kept her warm and dry. She reflected on the merits of dwarven manufacture. They really did make the best stuff.

This made her to think about the different races. Elves were not as numerous, yet they were the most magically adept, and so dominated the continent. Humans were numerous and tough, as she well knew. The alliance between elf and dwarf had always kept them in their frigid homeland, but it was a close thing.

Even caprans had their advantages. They were as strong and as hardy as the goats they were kin to. On a good day a capran sorceress was even a match for an elven mage.

The halflings, however.

She knew she shouldn't look down on them, they were as worthy as any other group of humanoids—but it was hard not to pity them. They were so puny, so short-lived, so completely unmagical. No wonder everyone called them *halflings*. They seemed only half-alive.

Someone tapped on the tent flap. The sound made her jump. "It's me," said Feanaro.

"Come in." She put away her journal and her second-in-command entered.

She looked at the man. Feanaro had silver hair and light blue skin, a common enough combination. He was handsome in an earnest way. He didn't usually look so calculating.

"You wanted something?" she asked.

He smirked. "I was going to ask you that."

"I'm fine," she said. "Thanks for your concern."

"Are you sure?" he said. He fingered the tent flap. "Remarkable thing, this dwarf-made tent. You have only to throw it to the ground and peg it down. Does this remind you of anything?"

"I'm sure I don't know what you mean?"

He grinned. "I was just thinking our fearless leader didn't get to have fun back in town. I thought, maybe I could help her with that."

She suppressed a shiver. "No, you may not. I wish you to leave my domicile now."

"Are you sure? Nobody ever needs to know."

"Get. Out."

"Okay, okay, I'm going. Good night, milady." He left.

Meerwen fastened the tent flap and sealed it with a glyph. She was shaking.

Drystone Under Siege

My aide-de-camp shook me awake. "Prince Angrod, you're needed at the front!"

I groaned. I'd barely gotten any sleep and still ached from the last battle.

I got up anyway and checked my bandaged torso. No bleeding, which meant the stitches were holding. I would've preferred a few minutes with a competent healer, but water mages were in short supply. I shrugged and allowed my aide to help me into my armour.

"Where is it this time?" I asked.

"The Manufacturing Quarter. The enemy has forced a landing and is fighting in the streets." She grimaced. "If they establish a presence there, they'll cut the city in half."

"And I'm the only mage on hand." I shook my head. The war was less than a year old and we'd lost so many people.

She fastened the left greave and stepped back. "Done, sir."

"Right." I marched into the next room, where my bodyguard awaited. They were all elven knights except for Heronimo.

"The enemy has landed their heavy assets here," he said, pointing to a spot on the map. "They are using them to support an infantry advance."

"What forces do we have in place?" I asked.

"Only the city guard. They're being pushed back."

"I'd like to land on top of the enemy, but that might confuse the militia. We teleport among them and do a frontal assault." I looked to my aide. "Pass the word."

While she addressed a scrying pool, the dozen or so knights checked their weapons. Arrows were counted. Swords slid into scabbards. The men scowled as they checked the fit of their armour.

"We've done this before, gentlemen," I said. "A quick strike to break their momentum and we can let the grunts mop up."

"We're with you, Angrod," Heronimo said. "Say the word."

We teleported into battle.

I don't know what was louder, the screaming, or our enemies' weapons. The firing was intense. The bigger guns only made it worse.

Back at the palace I'd drained the local magic field, so I had plenty of juice. First thing I did was throw an air shield over my men and the city guard. The shield was thousands of random air pockets, enough to deflect small-arms fire. I used more air magic to roar, "DEFENDERS OF DRYSTONE. FORWARD."

As one, we climbed over the barricades and charged the cannon. BOOM. It filled the air with hardwood bullets. I poured energy into our shields and they missed us, mostly. One hit a knight square in the breastplate. It punched through the armour and exploded out the back, spattering the men behind him. Another bullet glanced past my cheek.

"Forward!"

I drew my sword and held it high. Sparks leaped as the energy gathered. With a sweep of my arm I lashed my foes with *fire*.

The first ranks screamed. They had become living torches. They thrashed and ran, but then BOOM. The men behind them fired, smashing their burning comrades to the ground. An officer stepped forward, pistol high and sword out. "For the Emperor!"

He ran to meet me. Steel met red-hot steel as we parried and struck. He fired his pistol under my chin but I turned my head. I chopped down with my sword, drew the mace from my belt, and broke his jaw.

"For Brandish!" I said. The enemy infantry had closed to bayonet range. Heronimo leaped in front of me, his longsword opening throats and hacking down gun barrels. My men ducked under the bayonets with their bucklers raised, then came up swinging. The city guard threw themselves into the brawl.

The ironclads offshore decided to focus on us. A cannonball slammed into a balcony, showering us with debris. Another turned a group of militia into bone splinters.

"What I wouldn't give for a tame kraken," I said.

The nearest ship fired a broadside. The cannonballs arced toward us. I raised both arms and *pushed*. The cannonballs looped in the air. They slammed into masts and exploded on deck. One smashed below the waterline and the fighting ship began to sink.

"That should keep them busy," I said, but the infantry had rallied around another sword-swinging officer. He had an awesome moustache and a heavy arm. "For the Emperor!" he said, battering at my defence.

Not to be outdone, I poured energy into my sword and said, "For Brandish!"

"For the Emperor!"

"For Brandish!"

"For the Emperor!"

"For Brandish!"

"For the Emperor!"

"For DA EMPRAH."

"For Bran—*d'oh!*"

"Haha, gotcha!" I cut through his blade like an incandescent knife through butter. I beheaded him on the return stroke, then began swinging the electrified mace.

"How you doing, brother?" I called to Heronimo.

"Not bad," he said. "But we should probably withdraw."

"Now? But we're having so much fun!"

Heronimo didn't answer. A sniper had shot him in the head. The copper nail in the bullet had sent skull fragments tumbling through his brain. He was dead as he fell.

The dragons swept down and spat liquid fire.

They flew low, vomiting napalm over fortifications and troops. They screeched as they passed overhead and I wished I could summon lightning. Unfortunately I was out of power.

"Okay, Cruix, you win this time."

The dreams had been getting worse. Cruix was gaining ground. More and more I found myself fighting a losing cause. But then, when the objective is your own life, I really didn't have any other choice.

You can only stay awake for so long. I was running on coffee and naps, which left me feeling itchy. As if my skin didn't quite fit. As if my eyes weren't quite processing. Several times I thought I glimpsed Cruix laughing from the shadows—but it would take an awfully big shadow to hide a dragon.

We stayed in Zith'ra a few days to recuperate and see the sights. The king was generous with his time and we could not have had a better guide. I was struck by how much the city resembled Corinthe. The architecture was completely different (caprans tended to build rambling earthen palaces, no two alike) but still I was struck by how well the different quarters lined up. It was as if I were halfway to being a resident. I asked Arawn why this was so and he said it was due to the geographical similarities between our world and his.

"This is, after all, a fine place for a city. There is the sea and there is the forest. Your elven ancestors and our centaur forebears had the same idea."

It would have been pleasant to stay in Zith'ra until the end, but I had a need to die in my own bed. I said as much to Arawn.

"I understand," he said. "Let me escort you to the nearest fairy ring."

We rode to a clearing outside the city. Arawn told us to enter the circle conveniently marked by toadstools.

"It was good to meet you, Angrod, Heronimo, and Mina. As a gift, I give you the horses you now ride— finer animals have not been bred."

"Thank you, your majesty," I said. "I look forward to meeting you again, and to fulfilling our bargain."

The king smiled. "May Fortuna smile upon you."

He and his retinue rode around the fairy ring. They galloped and then disappeared. The constellations changed and we were back in our world.

In Corinthe Citadel, people had gathered to watch the show.

"Testing for First Lieutenant will commence!" bellowed a portly sergeant. "Spellcasting is allowed! Healers are on hand! You will match yourselves against

Captain Dinendal, recently returned from a special mission."

Dinendal leaned against a fence, eyes almost closed. He wore cavalry boots and a leather vest. His shirt billowed under the vest and his golden hair spilled over his shoulders. He had a pair of swords strapped to his back.

"Now, the captain might *look* like a good-for-nothing pretty boy, but make no mistake: he's one of the finest swordsmen in Brandish. In fact, we don't expect anyone to beat him! Just put up a fight!"

It was noon. Nearly all of the city guards were there. Some wanted to take the ranking exam, but most simply wanted to watch. To get ahead in the militia you had to be among the best, and not many were up to the challenge. There were few rules in these combat trials. Killing blows were forbidden, but accidents happened.

Dinendal didn't move, though his head dropped a little. He seemed to be dozing.

"Come now! Is no one brave enough to step into the ring with our captain?"

A hulking elf climbed over the fence. "I'll do it."

Dinendal opened an eye.

The challenger was tall—he towered head and shoulders over the captain. Dinendal himself was tall, which meant the other elf was very tall. He had broad shoulders too, and his arms rippled with muscle.

"Somebody's been hitting the weights," Dinendal said. "What's your name, kid?"

"I'm Veryan. I've been waiting to take down a smug bastard like you." He flexed his arms and the veins popped. "I've been lifting and running for years. Nobody can match my strength and stamina!"

"I hope you've put as much time into your bladework, or this will be short."

Veryan grinned. He drew his weapons, a short sword and buckler. "Captain, I will beat your arse and wipe that smile off your face!"

"Not with the same hand, I hope. Just attack already."

Veryan charged. He was shockingly fast. The captain didn't move at all. At the last moment he blinked away and Veryan slammed into the fence. The crowd laughed. Dinendal had reappeared in the centre of the arena. He still hadn't drawn his swords.

"Are we fighting for points?"

Veryan roared and came in swinging, but each time found only air. Dinendal teleported effortlessly from each attack, sometimes reappearing *behind* the sword stroke so it seemed to have passed through him. The crowd gasped. Plenty of elves could teleport, but few could do it so precisely or so often. Veryan tried to get the captain with the backswing but Dinendal got behind Veryan and tapped on his shoulder.

"HYAA!" Veryan said, turning and striking at once. The sudden inrush of air told him the captain had blinked away again.

A sweating Veryan raised his guard and stepped forward. He made a half-hearted swing—and was shocked when steel met steel. Dinendal had drawn a sword and parried Veryan's blade.

"Well, this *is* a swordfight," the captain said. He drew his other sword and widened his stance. "No more teleports!"

He unleashed a dazzling attack, a flurry of slashes and cuts that pushed Veryan back and made the crowd gasp. Dinendal's twin sabres flashed and weaved. No one could see an opening in his defence. Veryan fought desperately, trying to regain the initiative. He led with his buckler, the small shield like a metal fist. The blow would have ended the fight, but Dinendal sidestepped and kicked him in the head. Then the captain flicked out a sword and caught his arm.

"I have first blood," he said.

Veryan stumbled back. The captain was playing with him and he knew it. He decided to taunt the man. "You should be in the royal guard!" he said, grinning. "So why aren't you?"

"I like where I am," Dinendal said.

"Maybe you're as common as mud!" Veryan said, and a sword hilt hit him in the temple and he crashed to his knees. It was all he could do not to pass out. Dazed, he cried out as his weapons were slapped away and another pommel cracked two ribs. The air rushed from his lungs and he fell on his face, gasping. A booted heel broke his back and a kick broke his jaw. Veryan saw his teeth on the sand and then he blacked out.

"Healers here!" Dinendal said.

"Damn," the sergeant said. "That's going to take all night to repair."

"He'll live," the captain said, accepting a cup of water. He scanned the crowd and saw that the guardsmen had gone pale. "Who's next?" he called out.

Chapter 21

"Those were the shortest officer trials in decades," the sergeant said as the crowd dispersed. "Did you have to be so thorough?"

Dinendal sipped something stronger than water. "There's always next year. It's not like we're at war."

"Can I have your autograph, Dinny?"

"Sure, I—*Roddy?!*"

I hugged my childhood friend. It might have been strange for Heronimo and Mina to see me embrace such a brutal swordsman, but I'd grown up with Dinendal. We'd bloodied each other's noses often enough that I had no fear of him.

"It's good to see you," he said. "So you finally tore yourself from your studies?"

"Yes, finally," I said. "I've come home."

I stepped away and motioned to my companions. "This is Mina and Heronimo. I couldn't have gotten here without them."

"Roddy always did make interesting friends." His eyes narrowed. "Are you adventurers, by any chance?"

"We are," Heronimo said. "I am searching for the man who killed my parents. Like you, he is a dual-wielder of great skill. I have trained twenty years to meet him as equals."

"A worthy cause. And you, my dear? Are you also seeking vengeance?"

Mina looked a little awestruck—Dinendal was handsome, even for an elf. "Actually, I was just bored."

Dinendal laughed. "Well, and who hasn't wished for more excitement?"

We swept out of the citadel and into the city, talking the whole time.

Corinthe much resembled Drystone in design and beauty. Like the capital, the northernmost elven city had wide roads, spacious walkways, and graceful street lamps. There was one main difference, however:

"Angrod, it's snowing, isn't it?" Mina asked. The flakes were drifting down. "Then why don't I see any of it on the ground?"

She crouched. The streets were paved with red tiles. Whenever a snowflake touched one, it began to melt. She looked up at the roofs—they too were covered in red tiles. Downspouts conveyed the meltwater to the gutters.

"It's as if it were merely raining," she said.

"That would be the vinyrral tiles," I said. "They stay the same temperature as long as they're connected. Go ahead, touch one."

Mina pulled off a glove and touched a line of tiles. "It's hot!" she said.

"The tile network stretches deep underground, where the earth is molten. In the summer they reroute the circuit to tiles at the bottom of the sea, so Corinthe is comfortable year-round."

"Amazing!" Mina said.

"We aren't like you dwarves, who don't notice the weather underground," said Dinendal. "Neither are we like you humans, who don't notice the weather at all."

We walked past a park where two sets of tiles had been places so that some parts were grass and others sparkling snow. We paused to watch children make a snowman. When it was complete they carried it to a heated lawn to watch it slump.

"I'm melting! Melting!" said a young elf.

"Oh, what a world, what a world!" said another. "You've KILLED MEEE."

"Kids and their games," Dinendal said. "Takes me back."

We passed through the Old Quarter, which enjoyed trade with the northern human cities and the nearby capran capital. I'd always wondered how close Zith'ra was, but I'd never imagined the two cities were on top of one another.

Though I had recently passed through similar streets, it was still good to see my fellow elves. They shopped for furs and enjoyed themselves in the wine houses and pubs. It was the beginning of winter but many windows boasted flowers in vinyrral planters.

"It's good to be home," I said.

"You're not there yet," Dinendal said, and it was a few minutes before we arrived at my ancestral house.

All the mansions in the Palace Quarter were impressive, but Veneanar Castle trumped them all. It had a moat, for one thing—the castle seemed to float over a vast reflecting lake. Next to *that*, all the other homes seemed too small and close together.

"You live in a castle?" Heronimo asked.

"Grew up in one," I said. "The castle itself is one of the oldest buildings in Corinthe."

"I can make out stonework," Mina said. "I thought elves didn't use masonry."

"It was built by the earliest elves. They hadn't mastered magic and the crystal laminate was added later. All this land was ours before it was the Palace Quarter."

We walked down the bridge to the gatehouse, where I called out, "Uncle Erumaren! Auntie Marilla! I'm ho-oome!"

Something stirred, and then an ancient elf peered down from the parapet. "Why, it's Master Angrod! Come and see, Marilla!"

An equally ancient woman stuck her head between two merlons. She goggled at us. "Why, so it is! Welcome home! Welcome!"

They bustled down the stairs. They raised the first portcullis and opened the massive main gate, which swung soundlessly inward.

"It's good to see you again, young master!"

"Thank you, uncle," I said, shaking his hand. "I see you've kept the gates well-oiled."

"But of course," he said. "It's the least I could do."

He led us into the passage. Aunt Marilla dashed forward to embrace me. "Oh, Master Angrod, I thought I'd never see you again!"

I hugged her. "I always said I'd come home, and I have. These are my friends."

We made our introductions and the caretakers raised the second portcullis. We walked into the castle courtyard.

It was like walking into a field. Grass grew thickly between the paving stones. There were flowers, and field mice, and a hawk that preyed on the field mice. It nested in one of the trees. That's right, *trees*. They stood in the southwest corner, a little grove where the guards had once drilled.

"We kept your rooms like they used to be, milord," said Uncle Erumaren, "but as per your orders the rest of the castle is untouched."

"I didn't want to overwork you," I said. "It took a small army to maintain this place. The dusting alone was a full-time job."

"Will you be staying long?"

"As long as I can," I said. My two retainers didn't catch the note of sadness—they started talking among themselves.

"Is there enough food and drink in the buttery? The young master will require fine wines and meats!"

"I haven't gone shopping yet!"

I handed them my purse. "Please buy whatever you need with this," I said. "I will go and inspect my chambers."

"Ooh, he's acting all lordly," Dinendal said. "Did living in Drystone do that? Was it all the fish?"

"Are you related?" Mina asked.

Dinendal smiled. "We grew up in this same castle. As for being related, I wouldn't know—I never had any relatives. Angrod's aunt took me in as a baby and made me the stable boy."

"I'm sorry." Mina said.

"Don't be. I learned a lot about horses."

I walked into the household apartments, which were just as I remembered. Lots of heavy furniture, red velvet, and marble busts. Loads of gilt-frame paintings and weapons on the walls. Apparently my ancestors never wanted to be more than a few feet from a mace or battle-axe. In a pinch, you could use the sculptures in a fight.

"I like the décor," Heronimo said. "Very cosy."

"I knew you'd say that," Mina said. "It's like this place never knew a woman's touch."

"Actually, these used to be Aunt Arcalima's apartments. She sure loved her heirlooms."

We wandered the rambling old place. Much effort had gone into making it habitable but there was no disguising its original warlike purpose. The only natural light was from arrow-slits. The chandeliers hung from murder holes.

"Those are massive light fixtures," Mina said.

"They're designed to drop onto intruders," I said. "That's why the spikes."

"Oh," she said. She and Heronimo took a few steps to the side.

"You can see why I wanted to get away," I said. "House Veneanar has always produced administrators and military leaders. Laid-back types like me, not really."

"And yet you have returned," Dinendal said.

"A man ought to die at home, in his own bed."

His eyebrows shot up. "You seem healthy from where I'm standing."

"You might want to sit down."

We found the main hall and sat at the long table, where I once again recounted the events leading to that moment. We'd found my aunt's liquor stash and were enjoying ice wine, a Corinthe specialty. It tasted like candy.

"So this dragon is going to take over your body and erase your mind like a blackboard? And you're going to let him?"

"Pretty much. I can't do anything to threaten him." I described how Cruix was like a spreading infection. "As it is, he's content to let the process happen gradually. He says it's inevitable and I believe him. Fighting would only shorten my remaining time."

"What can we do?"

"Just stay out of his way. He only wants to go into the wilderness, away from humanoid civilization."

"How much longer—?" Mina asked.

I took a sip of wine. "Days."

Uncle and Auntie arrived with a huge roast ham, a wheel of Corinthan cheese, and loaves of good white bread. The ham dripped with maple syrup and the cheese was fresh and strong.

"My favourite foods," I said. "Uncle, Auntie, please join us."

"We wouldn't presume," Uncle said. "Marilla and I have our own dinner waiting at the gatehouse. Please don't hesitate to ring." And they bowed out of the great hall.

"There go some perfect house elves," said Dinendal, shaking his head. "And to think I almost became a butler."

"Instead you became a swordsman, and a good one," Heronimo said.

"They didn't make it easy. My first and second choices were royal guardsman and combat mage, but you need a pedigree for either of those. As a foundling, I had to make do with the city guard."

"It can't be that bad," I said.

"The regular army calls us weak-end soldiers." Dinendal took a drink. "They also call us the Teatime Army, because we're always home in time for tea."

He took another drink. "The royal guard gets better pay and better equipment. Anybody with the tiniest bit of pull signs up with them. The city guard, meanwhile, is full of the old and the weak. The shabby and the shoddy. We're the dregs *under* the barrel."

"But you're one of the best swordsmen I've ever seen!" Heronimo said.

"Too right I am," Dinendal said. "Unfortunately, people think I have halfling blood. It's in the ears, see? Not quite as pointy."

I looked at my friend. His clothes fit him so well they had to be tailored. Expensive, but not obviously so, which made them even more valuable. "You seem to do okay," I said.

"I find side jobs. I still wouldn't have a regular job if ancient law didn't call for a militia."

"How did you learn your skills?" Heronimo asked.

"I was Angrod's sparring partner. Took it much more seriously than he did, let me tell you. Later I met as many masters as I could. I learned a trick here, a technique there. I never had a proper teacher, but studied constantly."

Heronimo leaned forward. "Surely you know the best dual-wielders in the land."

"That I do. But first, why you are seeking a certain swordsman?"

Heronimo explained how he came to be on his quest. "… and so I seek justice for my murdered village."

Dinendal leaned back, boots on the table. "How could I refuse? There's no justice in the world."

"Too right," Heronimo said, and they brought their glasses together.

Dinendal sat up and drew closer to my human friend. "Can you remember anything else about this mass-murdering elf? What did his weapons look like?"

"They were curved swords, like yours…" Heronimo said, "… but the blades were like shark's teeth."

"Ah-ha!" Dinendal said. "That could only be Serrato Alva. The Pirate Perverse, as he is known, wears midriff-baring armour and fights like a dancing girl. An extremely dangerous man all the same."

"And you know him?"

"Know him? He gave me this!" Dinendal raised his shirt to show a long scar under his right rib. "Something to remember him by. He can be found on the sea route between Drystone and Dragons Claw. If you like, I can help you find him."

"Can you?" Heronimo said, almost leaping out of his chair.

"Certainly. I'm only on duty one weekend a month."

Chapter 22
The Last Stand of Angrod Veneanar

I fell from the battlements and the enemy slithered over the walls. I drew sword and mace and swung them in lethal arcs but they kept on coming. Beside me, my doubles did no better.

There was the Fool, who cackled and thrashed. He looked like I did as a teenager and his weapon was a teddy bear. It was covered with spikes and impaled on a stick. There was the King, an older version of me. His hair was gray but he wore plate armour and wielded a longsword with ease. Next to him was the Queen—me as a woman—who jabbed at the enemy with her spear.

The enemies were already dead, but that didn't stop them. They came over the walls, bloodless and decayed, their eyes unblinking. They staggered toward us and we cut them down. We slashed them and hammered them and still they took ground. Inch by jagged inch.

"Duck!"

We crouched and fire flew over our heads.

The Magus crackled with power, his red robes scorched and smoking. He triggered a glyph and swept the horde with focused hellfire. The Priestess supported him with arrows of light. The Hermit had thrown his beard over his shoulder and was calling down lightning with his liver-spotted arms.

They all wore my face. They all were me. And yet we were not enough. Veneanar Castle was nearly overrun. We'd blown the bridge but the enemy had filled the moat with bodies. The ramp? More bodies.

I stabbed upward and caught a zombie under the chin. I planted a boot in him and pushed him off, then slapped his hands aside with my mace. The flanged head swung back and knocked off the zombie's jaw. I cut low and gutted him, then caved in his face. "Come on! *Come on!*"

"Don't encourage them!"

I slipped on an intestine and a zombie lunged. I brought up my right arm and its teeth cracked on solid silver. I raised the arm and the Priestess shot it in the eye.

"Low on arrows!"

"Just use mana!"

"Low on that too!"

We'd been fighting for hours. The worst part was that the corpses were getting more familiar. I was sure I'd just clubbed my next-door neighbour.

Elrond lurched into view. "Master Angrod. Surprised to see me?"

I raised my weapons, but hesitated. That was enough for the zombies to grab me. Their stinking bodies bore me to the ground. I held my breath and called on the fire. My back grew red hot, then hotter still. The zombies caught fire. *Hotter*. I poured energy into the spell-glyph and the bodies were cremated in an instant.

I straightened, ashes pouring off my back.

"Way to go, me!" said the Magus. "We'll make a wizard out of you yet!"

"Look out!"

I ducked, but the longsword trimmed my hair. I turned and saw Heronimo. His brains were leaking out his ears.

That didn't hurt his swordsmanship one bit. He cut with no wasted effort—I frantically parried.

"I'll handle this," said the King. He advanced with his visor down and his guard up. Blade met blade and manoeuvred for advantage. They fenced. Heronimo lunged, angling for a stab, but the King parried and slid his sword over Heronimo's, the edge rising to meet the zombie's throat. Heronimo turned his head but still lost his helmet to the upward stroke. The King went for a thrust but his opponent parried. He twisted his blade and lunged, the sword point slipping between the human's ribs.

Heronimo looked at the sword. "I'm dead, remember?" He beat aside the King's blade and landed a ringing blow on the King's helmet.

They fought on. Both were masters of the longsword. Their blades whittled the air, the points dancing between them. They used their swords as levers and dealt measured cuts. One would take a hand off his sword to grab or punch. Pommels were thrust into faces and crossguards used as hammers. The King tried to sever nerves and tendons. Heronimo tried to crush armour or strike an unprotected spot. When a zombie got in their way they cut it down without a glance. The air filled with the rasp and the clash of steel.

Heronimo grasped his own blade in one hand and thrust it into the King's visor, piercing an eyehole. The King's sword clattered on the stones. Heronimo reversed his sword and battered the King's helmet with the crossguard. Once, twice, and the King fell, blood streaming from his helmet.

Heronimo let his sword slip from his hands. The cuts on his palms and fingers were bloodless. The bone was showing and the dead flesh wasn't healing at all. My former friend looked at his hands and cursed. "Well, fuck me."

The Magus snapped his fingers. Air rushed into Heronimo's ears and popped his skull open.

Cruix landed on the Magus, the Priestess, and the Hermit, pulping them. He lashed his tail and reared. "Mind if I drop in?" he rumbled.

"Oh gods you actually said that."

He took a breath and I threw myself from the walls. He swept the Queen and the Fool with liquid fire.

The next thing I knew, I was being passed from hand to hand. There was a gallows in the courtyard.

"Hello, my apprentice."

Valandil was a charred and leathery ruin. He was more meat than man and I only recognized him by his voice. "Do you like my gallows?" he asked. "I used the trees from that corner. I thought we'd send you off in style."

"You're too kind," I said. I considered the wooden frame. "Clean lines, classical proportions, looks like a wedding arch. You've outdone yourself."

Hands lowered me to my feet and held my arms behind me. They manhandled me up the steps and placed a noose around my neck. I stood over a trapdoor, so I searched for the lever—and found Mina already manning it.

"You too?" I said.

She smiled. She looked almost alive, except for the yawning hole in her chest. "Yes, me too. I wouldn't miss this for anything, Angrod. Not even death."

"What's it like?"

"You'll find out."

Cruix leaped from one of the towers, transforming as he landed. He stood before me as an elf, looking identical except for his hair. While mine was wavy and black his was white and straight. His armour was patterned after his scales.

"Today's the day," he said. "I win, you know. I've taken over your mind, layer by layer, level by level. I have usurped each of your body's functions. Soon every cell will belong to me."

"Just hang me already, you walking cancer."

"Mina?" Cruix said. "Do the honours."

She threw the lever back and the world fell out from under me. I tumbled into space—

—and onto the floor. Next to the bed. Goddamn it.

"You okay, Angrod?" Heronimo said.

"Did I sleep for a year or something? I feel weak."

"Just four hours. Isn't that enough?"

"An elf can go without sleep for a month," I said, as he helped me to my feet. "It doesn't do any favours for his sanity, though."

Mina walked in. "Things are about to get seriously crazy. Take a look at who's standing on the bridge."

We rushed to the walls. There on the bridge was an elf in a steel fox mask.

"It's him!" Heronimo said, drawing his sword. "My family's murderer!"

"Was he standing like that when you saw him?" I asked Mina. "Shoot between his feet."

She obliged. The crossbow bolt thunked into the planking.

The elf didn't move.

"Shoot over his shoulder."

The next bolt flew past his ear. Still no reaction. He could've been a statue except that his clothes moved with the wind.

There was no wind.

"Shoot him in the chest," I said.

Her shot was true. It hit him centre mass and buried itself in the bridge behind him.

"Wasn't *that* powerful," she said. "There's no blood."

"It's a sending," I said. "Just light and water."

We raised the outer portcullis and approached. We glanced left and right for ambush, weapons in hand.

"Nothing in the water," I said. "Nothing past the moat. It just wants to talk."

"Well, what do you want?" Heronimo yelled. "Face me in the flesh, coward!"

The elf chuckled. "Soon. Hey, Angrod, I've been on your trail for months. It's time you saw my face."

He took off his mask and it was Dinendal.

"I—what—Dinny—"

"*Don't you call me that.* We haven't been friends for a long time."

"I wrote, man. I sent packages. We grew up together!"

Dinendal sneered. "I assure you, we had different childhoods. I the pauper and you the prince—we were always meant to come to blows."

In my mind I flashed back to the boy who always smelled of horses and never put on weight, no matter how Auntie Marilla fed him. A wild, lonely boy who went anywhere he wanted. I used to envy him. But on the bridge, I realized he had been able to do anything he wanted because nobody cared.

"What happened to you?" I asked.

"I made my own way," he said. "I practiced the sword until someone noticed. Have some of you heard of the Elendil Order?"

Mina gasped. "The King's Assassins! My da, he knew of you!"

"*King's Assassins*. Heh. More like the King's Enemies. My dear, the Elendil Order exists to tear down the aristocracy, even if it occasionally involves working for them. For some time I had been looking forward to liquidating Angrod and his master."

"*You* slaughtered my people?" Heronimo asked.

"Yes, *I* was the monster. Did you recognize my style back at the boy's village? I don't think of it as making enemies, I think of it as giving me an exciting old age!" And he laughed.

Heronimo roared and struck, but sliced only water.

Dinendal smirked. "Turns out I could've been a mage, had I the opportunity. Watch this."

The moat erupted. Pillars of water fountained upward and hung over us like a cathedral ceiling.

Then the water fell and caught the light.

I blinked. It was Corinthe Citadel. The city guard was drilling in the courtyard. Three dozen spears and halberds were in ragged formation. No two weapons were alike. Their owners were too tall, too short, too fat, or too skinny. None of them was recruitment poster material. None had armour that fit. Most were only good for killing Saturday mornings and pints at the local tavern.

The fat old sergeant bellowed soundlessly. A youth dropped his halberd, bent to pick it up, and lost his helmet. Veryan scowled from the sidelines. He tried to slouch against a fence but his back brace got in the way.

They never had a chance.

The sergeant was a former royal guardsman. He was the most dangerous. Arrows hit him from all sides and a fireball blew his head off. More arrows fell upon the militia. They scattered in all directions.

Unfortunately, they were surrounded. Fox-faced killers dropped their cloaks and drew their weapons.

"This has already happened," Dinendal told us. "There's nothing you can do."

Another Dinendal strolled through the courtyard, pausing now and then to disarm a soldier or cripple him. Veryan put up a fight but was sliced into three pieces. A spearman lunged. Dinendal slashed and the spear became a stick. A halberdier brought his weapon down like an axe and the assassin parried. The spearman—now holding just a staff—attacked again.

Dinendal sidestepped and let the man take the halberd in the belly. Then he cut off the halberdier's arms.

Dinendal continued his walk. More assassins followed, finishing the wounded with captured spears.

"I took control of the Citadel half an hour ago," said the Dinendal on the bridge. "Unless you surrender, we will turn its catapults upon the city. Their stones could easily be enchanted to explode."

I laughed. "Why bother? I'm dying already. I'll be gone in a day or so."

Dinendal shook his head. "We want the dragon too. The prophecy will hang over our heads for as long as it lives." He smiled. "And if the thought of your city burning isn't enough, I have your girlfriend."

They'd thrown open the citadel gates to admit her. Meerwen was covered in bruises and chains. Half a dozen assassins dragged her along. Their boots were caked with muddy snow—so were her knees. She fell and nearly pulled them to the ground. Earth magic. Even thoroughly beaten, she was determined to make things difficult.

An Elendil assassin struck her head with the end of a spear. He hit her again, again, and only then did she go limp.

The scene collapsed. Water pattered into the moat and the surface grew still. I shook myself, but we were perfectly dry.

The sending of Dinendal remained. "You have one hour to show yourself. Come alone. If you don't I will cut off her limbs and nail her to the gates—and I guarantee she'll live long enough to feel it. Do you understand?"

I snarled. "I hear you!"

"Good. And Angrod? *I can see your house from here.*"

The catapult stone slammed into the moat and drenched us in what was essentially pond water.

"What an arsehole," Mina said.

Chapter 23

"Are you going?" she asked.

I thought about it. Cruix was fighting every inch of the way. It was like trying to juggle while wading through quicksand. The hammering in my head was so bad I could barely see. Still, I remained in control. The struggle shortened my time to mere hours, but I still had my own mind.

All this time I'd pitted my will to live against Cruix's. That hadn't worked too well. Cruix was older, more ruthless, and much more determined to survive. But sometimes dying well is more important than simple survival.

"I'll do it," I said. "If it's the last thing I do."

"Assault a fortress full of heavily-armed and magically-accomplished assassins?" Heronimo said. "You know it's a suicide mission, right?"

"Right."

"You also realize that anyone who goes with you is almost certainly doomed as well?" Mina said.

"Right," I said. "I go alone."

"No, you're not," she said.

"Wouldn't be a proper last stand without your true companions," he said

"I ordered adventure," Mina said. "I eat what I order and chew what I bite off."

"That's… probably more poetic in Dwarvish," I said.

Heronimo sheathed his sword. "Dinendal is *mine*. Any problems with that?"

"None. None at all."

We returned to the castle to prepare. Mina checked her panoply, making sure the various enchantments were in order. She filled her quiver and fastened her helmet.

Heronimo went bare-chested. He cut strips from the red velvet couches and tied them around his wrists, elbows, and shoulders.

"Tassels of power?" I asked.

"Tourniquets," he said.

Then he cut his palms, letting the blood pool in his hands. *Slap*. He marked his left breast with the imprint. *Slap*. The right breast. Then he brought bloody fingers to his face and painted there a bird of war.

"I'm ready," he said.

We gathered in the courtyard. It was a beautiful day.

"How are we getting to the citadel?" Mina asked. "Every approach will be watched."

"Not *every* approach," I said. "They forget, I grew up in Corinthe. I know it well."

"What's that got to do with—" Mina said, but Uncle Erumaren ran up. He wore armour and carried a spear and sword.

"Wait for me, young master!" he gasped. "I will fight by your side!"

I nearly cried. My old retainer's suit of mail was three sizes too large—it hung from his limbs and rustled mightily.

"I'm touched, uncle, but it's been a long time since you carried a sword. Let us young idiots handle the fighting."

Uncle Erumaren wept. "I have served your family all my life. Do you think I'd let it die out on my watch?"

I clapped his arm. "Very well, you shall lead the reinforcements. Contact Drystone, then rally the citizenry and attack the Citadel once the gates are down."

He nodded. "I won't fail you. But milord, you are not fully armed."

"What are you talking about? I've got my mace and my stick."

He snorted. "That stick? A training weapon!"

"I get that a lot."

He shook his head. "It's dangerous to go unarmed— take this." He pressed the sword into my hands. "Your uncle's. He made me keep it safe until the day a Veneanar would need it again."

I drew it from its scabbard. Dark blue steel glittered. The blade was wavy like a flame.

"Wicked!" Heronimo said.

I sheathed it and hung it from my belt. The stick I tossed into hammerspace. "Okay," I said. "Now I'm ready."

"So, how are we breaking into the fortress?" Heronimo asked.

"We're not going to break into the fortress," I said, grabbing his wrist.

"What then?" Mina said, as I grabbed her wrist.

"I'd hold hands if I were you two," I said. I tightened my grip on both of them. "You're going to love this— we'll simply drop in on them."

I closed my eyes, leaped into the air, and we disappeared.

We teleported into the sky over Corinthe. Mina screamed.

"We're FALLING, fools!"

Gravity took over. There was a sensation of dropping until air friction kicked in and caught us like a net. I grinned at my friends. *Relax.*

We spread out and became a flower in freefall. The wind rushed past our ears and buffeted our faces. It was impossible to talk. Maybe I should've given more warning. I shrugged and looked down.

Corinthe stretched under me. I knew every road and building. I knew them so well, in fact, that I'd been able to visualize them from two miles up. It was day, but I switched to my Sight to get a better feel for the city at night. It glowed. The Citadel, with its elevated position over Corinthe, was easy to spot. I began casting Featherfall to slow our descent.

They'll never see us coming, I thought.

Dinendal stood on the battlements and looked down at the main approach. The spy scanned the road for his childhood friend, but saw nothing.

"Is the prisoner secure?" he asked his aide.

"We've got her under guard in the dungeons, sir."

"Good. If I know Angrod, he'll try something. And even if he doesn't, there's still that dragon to think about."

"We've turned some of the ballistae toward the courtyard."

"Very good. Now if only the guest of honour could show up."

The breeze ruffled his hair. He frowned. That wasn't right. He looked around the fortress and saw every flag and banner flapping *inward*. Where was the wind going…?

He glanced upward and screamed. *"To arms! To arms!"*

We broke away from each other. We were still falling too fast so I called upon earth magic to harden our bodies. We smashed into the ground, shattering the flagstones. The last of the Featherfall spell gusted in all directions, kicking up dust.

Nobody moved. Our heads snapped up to look at the assassins. They stepped back. We rose and drew weapons.

"Mina, look for Meerwen in the dungeons. Heronimo? Avenge your family."

The Elendil Order unfroze. They shot arrows but I raised a shield of turbulent air and they missed by inches. Fireballs exploded at our feet.

I raised my flamberge blade and blasted back. Mina loosed bolt after bolt, drawing the crossbow one-armed with enhanced dwarven strength. She never paused to aim, but her shots flew straight and true.

A harpoon went past my knee and I looked to the walls. "The ballista crews! Take them out!"

I raised my mace and called down the lightning. BOOM. The world went white. A tower crumbled. More assassins rushed across the courtyard.

With a roar, Heronimo charged. He cut left and cut right and two elves fell in four pieces. He recovered, turned, and bisected an assassin from collarbone to crotch. The main group of assassins paused in shock. Mina drew axe and buckler. Her arms shook as the enchantments kicked in. "All right you fools! Fools and sons of fools! *Come and get it!*"

We ran and met our enemies. The world was a symphony of breaking bones and dying screams. Heronimo was covered in more blood now, none of it his own. He raised his sword and howled.

An assassin came at me with a warhammer. It was like a giant meat tenderizer and wondrously agile in his hands. I skipped back and it missed my ribs by an inch. I menaced him with the sword and checked his next swing with my mace. I deflected it to the ground and vomited fire in his face.

Mina fought without pattern, without rhythm. Her gear gave her greater strength, speed, and toughness. Her reflexes and fighting instinct were also enhanced. The buckler in her other hand was a flash of light. Her axe bit deep into armour and flesh.

"The keep!" I said. "Get to the keep!"

We fought through our enemies. Heronimo took an arrow in the shoulder but kept going. Another lodged in his thigh and he powered on. We'd landed close to the keep so Mina was soon pounding up the ramp. I called up my fighting stick and hurled it as hard as I could.

It tumbled end over end, reshaping itself in mid-flight. It glowed with power and struck like a thunderbolt. BOOM. The keep was open.

"Go! Go!" Heronimo said. We turned to our pursuers and kept them in the courtyard. Arrows, fireballs, and ballista bolts whistled over our heads.

"Getting hot," Heronimo said. "Too many mages spoiling the broth."

"I can do something about that," I said. "Goodbye, my friend. Be sure to get well clear."

"What are you—"

I threw my weapons aside and called upon the beast.

The transformation still hurt. A *lot*. Not as much as before, though, and it went faster. Whether I was getting better at it or whether Cruix had nearly won, I chose not to wonder. I just let my bones stretch and my muscles swell. My features contorted and my jaws grew toothy. Organs expanded while others disappeared. New structures appeared out of formless tissue. Arrows and fireballs pattered on my hide.

I grew massive. I grew huge. I drained all the magic for miles. The lights went out across the city. A fountain exploded, spattering bystanders in icy water.

In Corinthe Citadel, all the combat mages gestured uselessly, their mana pools exhausted. On the other hand, I was now a full-grown dragon.

"Party!"

I charged the Elendil. My tail lashed out, flicking one into a wall and impaling another on its spikes. I backhanded an assassin over the battlements, then grabbed another and squeezed him to pulp. I slapped one so hard his legs fell off.

Yes! Yes! KILL.

Cruix shouted encouragement. I could feel him trying to take over, so we compromised. I leaped into the air and he loosed a fiery blast. He kicked out with our legs and I pounded an elf flat with a front paw.

Two minds. Six limbs. *Of course* we were a killing machine.

We were having an indecent amount of fun when the ballistae started shooting.

Picture a crossbow. Make it so large that no single man can lift it. Mount it on wheels, replace every wooden part with steel, and make it so powerful it takes a winch to draw back. What you have now is a siege weapon more than capable of punching through dragon hide.

They hit us in the neck, the flank, and the wing. Cruel barbs caught in our flesh and we roared. More harpoons came and we found ourselves trapped. We tried breathing fire, but had run out of mana.

They put harpoons into its limbs. They pulled the chains taut and staked them down. They reloaded the ballistae. As they had done a thousand times before, they subdued a dragon with numbers and steel.

"Nice work, men," Dinendal said. "We've nailed it down like a circus tent."

The beast still lived though. Pierced in a dozen places, bleeding and spurting onto the stones, it refused to die. The assassins had thrown nets and chains over its head so it could hardly move. Its legs, wings, and tail were stretched as though upon a rack. It was helpless.

The Elendil kept their distance all the same.

"How much longer?" asked Dinendal.

His aide snapped his fingers and produced a flame. "Soon. The magic is returning. It will power our death spells before long."

"That was rather anticlimactic. Somehow I was expecting more of a fight."

"I—I seem to be impaled."

A huge sword was sticking out of his belly. As Dinendal watched, his aide was lifted off his feet and carelessly dumped over the swordsman's back.

"Hello, Dinny," said Heronimo.

Mina was in the keep when the lights flickered. She was dragging her axe through someone's guts when her senses dulled and her limbs grew heavy.

"Oh, no," she said. An assassin jabbed at her with a spear. It caught her in the chest. The chain mail held but she backpedalled, shocked. "I felt that!"

She struck wildly and severed the man's fingers. He shrieked and she followed with a cut to the neck. He died, but her gear wasn't working anymore. "Damn it to hell!" she said. She could hear more enemies running down the stairs. She could flee to the dungeon, but she'd be trapped.

Or would she?

She ran deeper underground and smashed the gas lanterns. Soon it was completely dark. She got out her crossbow and waited at the foot of the stairs.

The dungeon door was kicked open. "It's dark! Get a lamp!"

She fired. At that range, she couldn't miss.

Smashing glass. "She's shooting the lamps!"

"No shit, really?"

"Get down there! She's as blind as we are!"

Pounding feet. They shut the door behind them, making the darkness complete. So of course she tripped them.

"Ouch!"

"Get your bearings! Remember, we trained for this. Fighting blind is nothing new for the Elendil Order."

Mina triangulated and struck.

"Aaargh!"

"You forget, boys, you're fighting a dwarf. I grew up underground."

Chapter 24

"I am Heronimo, son of Hrascar and Grimalda. Prepare to die!"

The elves moved toward him, but Dinendal held out his hand. "No one interfere. This one's mine."

He drew his twin blades. The serrated edges caught the light. He let his arms fall to his sides, then crossed them over his chest in a salute.

With both hands, Heronimo raised his longsword so he could almost kiss the blade. He looked over the crossguard, then lifted the weapon over his head.

Dinendal smiled. "So you think you're the man to kill me? You think you're good enough?"

"I ought to be, after twenty years."

Every assassin burst out laughing. Dinendal smirked. "Heh. I'm sure that's a long time for a human, but among elves, twenty years is nothing."

"If that's true, how did I kill so many of you?"

Silence. Dinendal scowled. "Okay, you have some skill. But now you're facing *me*."

They had begun to circle, the human and the elf. The other assassins backed away.

"Twenty years," Dinendal said. He grinned. "We spend that many years just laying the foundations? We go through *decades* of juggling and acrobatics before we even pick up a wooden waster."

"What is this, clown school?"

"Hah! Many times I considered running away. But I was patient, as an elf should be, and in time I saw the point of all that foolish training."

He drew his swords and twirled them. "The swords that killed your father, boy. See them fly!" He threw them up into the air, only to catch them and again.

"This isn't a game!" Heronimo said. "Defend yourself!"

"Watch this."

As Dinendal juggled his swords he drew a dagger and passed it from hand to hand so it tumbled from left to right. His hands blurred and then there were two daggers. "I could do this all day," he said, as he manipulated the steel cascade. He threw the blades and caught them, caught them and threw them. He plucked them from the air and let them hang in space.

"Enough!" Heronimo said, starting to lunge. He staggered back with knives in his chest.

Dinendal twirled his sabres. "If there's anything a performer hates, it's being interrupted. Prepare to die, art hater!"

Fighting in the dark. Blind, and trying not to breathe loudly. Everyone had stripped off their armour—even chainmail rustled too loudly. They shuffled in the dark, weapons ready.

Mina kept her mouth open, the better to hear with. Someone coughed and she lashed out, splitting someone's skull. She stepped away as the man fell. Someone cursed and she threw the axe, which made a meaty *thunk*. She drew her knife and continued to stalk her enemies.

I lay on the flagstones, weighted with chains, hooks digging into my flesh. I breathed, and I bled, and I slipped away from the world.

No! This isn't happening! I have not begun to live!

I would have smiled, had I a face. "Tough shit, Cruix. Looks like I'm taking you with me."

NO!

"It's too bad so much magical lore has been lost. I would've liked to know how the old wizard planned to resurrect you."

There was a meaningful silence.

"Wait, do you know? After all this time?!"

I would have preferred to overwrite your mind, but there is an alternative. It is painful, risky, and likely to lead to our death. You won't like it at all. Nevertheless, it's better than certain death.

"Tell me!"

First I need some promises from you.

They were things I could live with—provided I survived. I agreed, and he told me.

He was right, I didn't like it at all.

There was a way to turn nonliving matter into living matter. You needed a natural talent for transmutation. Dragons, who turned their stomach contents into napalm, had that talent. Then, also, you needed certain insights. Having shapeshifted beyond the dreams of any water mage, I had that insight.

In our head Cruix droned an ancient chant. This focused our mind and I began to glimpse the great source of magic deep beneath our feet. I had the impression of a massive, all-seeing eye gazing out from the centre of the world. And I knew that, if I were brave enough—if I were strong enough—I could call upon it directly.

I could power the working. All I needed now was enough organic matter to shape into a new body.

I raised my right arm and bit into it.

"Dual-wielders use each weapon independently. Novices act like they're swinging chairs around."

The fight had not gone well for Heronimo. Twenty-three times they had crossed swords and twenty-three times he had been bloodied. For all his strength and reach, he was completely outmatched. The elven assassin was simply the best swordsman he'd ever met. No matter how Heronimo cut and lunged, Dinendal parried with a minimum of effort, all while lecturing.

"A common mistake is to block with both weapons. You often see that in stage fighting because crossed swords look cool. Tell you the truth, a single weapon can deflect virtually all attacks. Using *two* wastes effort and opens holes in your defence. For instance, if I cut high like so, you naturally raise your guard and—hah! —leaves you open to a belly slash."

Heronimo retreated, holding his belly together.

"I notice you aren't healing. Could it have something to do with the depleted magic field?"

"At least you can't teleport away, *coward!*"

Dinendal laughed. "I don't need magic to finish you off!"

He unleashed a series of techniques that drove Heronimo against the wall and left his flesh in strips. The elf flicked the blood from his swords and smiled.

"That bit where you spin around and pretend you're a circular saw? Ridiculous. Doing that on the battlefield is asking to be stabbed in the back. Tell you the truth, dual-wielding isn't suited for war, where a good shield is better than a secondary weapon. Only in the hands of a duellist or ambush predator do twin blades really shine."

Heronimo went on the offensive but every attack was intercepted. Worse, each one was met with an attack of its own as Dinendal's swords wove in and out of his guard. Heronimo would block a sword, only to have the other strike from nowhere. He used the longsword's reach but Dinendal lunged from odd angles. The elf cut low and the human hobbled away.

"Did I get you in the knee?" Dinendal said, blades twirling. "Sorry. Guess you're only good for the city guard now."

Heronimo felt dizzy. His skin was flayed in places and blood pulsed from deep cuts. Still he fought, drawing upon a lifetime of rage. He roared and swung, trying to overpower the elf's skill. "Just—shut—up—!"

"Uh oh, he's getting his second wind," Dinendal said. "As I was saying, while it's impractical to defend with both weapons, it's all right to attack with both weapons from two different angles. When you trap an opponent's limb between two weapons, that's called a scissor's technique—"

His swords came together and cut off Heronimo's left hand.

"—can you guess why? Gentlemen, give the man a hand! He'd join in the applause, but he can't clap worth a damn!"

The assassin laughed. Bellowing, Heronimo tried to punch Dinendal with the stump, but the elf cartwheeled away, slashing twice. Heronimo's other hand sailed off the battlements with his longsword.

Dinendal roared with laughter. "This is so much fun! I really must massacre more villages."

Heronimo snarled. He raised the stumps to his face and tightened the tourniquets with his teeth. He growled, preparing to rush Dinendal. The elf took a step toward him—and the nearest assassin exploded in blood.

Try biting your wrist. Bite down hard enough to hurt. Bite down until you leave tooth marks in the skin, until you can't stand the pain anymore.

Now imagine not stopping. Imagine tearing into a hunk of raw meat, the flesh bloody and tough. Imagine that it's *your* flesh, that you can feel every one of your teeth as you tear chunks from yourself.

When you eat your own arm, expect pain.

Oh, gods the pain.

I gasped. Slobbered. Forced myself to swallow another mouthful. Fought to keep it down.

Come on, elf!

"I… can't…"

Come on, ELF.

I fainted several times, but always woke up. Cruix brought me back. Inside my head I wept, but he goaded me on.

Come on, stupid, I'm in pain too but I'm still—nngh —here. KEEP EATING.

I ate the meat, and tore the gristle, and crunched the bones. I ate until I swore I would never eat again.

Naturally, my captors noticed this.

"Is it—it's eating itself! Like a fox in a trap!"

"Ha! Nobody said dragons were too smart. Let the last of its kind die an animal!"

Nnn... no. I. Will. Not. Nngh.

I must have fainted again, because the next time I woke up the world was on fire.

Findecano Elanesse swooped out of the sky like a bat with a beard. Robes flapping, Dinendal's former master brought death wherever he looked. He would glance at an assassin and detonate their heart. The blood flashed to steam and the ribcage exploded, throwing bone shards in all directions. Findecano landed and three assassins rushed him. He summoned wind and threw them at the gates. They hit so hard the inner gate blew outward. A well-placed fireball and the outer gates were down. Armed townspeople streamed in. Royal guardsmen teleported onto the battlements.

It was a good time to run, but Dinendal still had the human to finish off. He looked to where Heronimo had been, but saw only a blood trail.

"Hey, where'd you go? We aren't done yet!"

He followed the trail. It disappeared up the stairs of the northwest tower.

"You think something there can save you? There's nothing but catapults! And even if there were weapons, you couldn't pick them up! Ha ha!"

He sheathed one blade and, sword in hand, began to climb the steps.

I awoke to a shower of scalding blood. What fresh sorcery was this?

Were my friends still alive?

Now or never. I closed my eyes and reached inside.

Centuries from now, historians would still argue over this moment. Was this when the elven race began its decline? Was this when the world began to change… for the better?

If I had known what I was setting in motion, would I have continued?

Only hindsight is perfect. In the moment, you act on what you know. I drew upon myself, focusing my entire being on a single point. I called up power from deep beneath earth, where rivers of iron flowed like water. I dipped into the vast molten currents, trying to bend them to my will. I was a leaf daring to steer an ocean.

But I had mind. I had leverage. The air hardened with potential.

Keep going, Cruix said.

With my Sight I visualized my old body. Two arms, two legs, upright posture. Quite attractive to the ladies. I saw its beating heart, saw blood coursing through arteries and veins. I saw the heart resting in a cage of bone. I recalled every system and held it in my mind. I remembered how they worked together.

Keep going.

I looked closer, down to the cellular level. The molecular level. I beheld the basis of heredity and glimpsed the forces behind elven longevity. Elegant, really. Dragons and elves were not so different—and a way to reconcile the two was suddenly clear.

Almost there.

I began to see double. I had turned my Sight inward and built a working model of my own brain, memories and all. It grew in complexity until there were four minds in the same skull—two of me and two of Cruix. At the signal, we pinched off parts of ourselves until only one of each remained.

There. There!

I opened my mouth and vomited fire.

"Come out, come out, wherever you are," Dinendal said. He paused. "I've always wanted to say that."

He continued to climb. He did so leisurely, for the steps were uneven by design. Anyone who didn't know the pattern would stumble if he ran. The staircase was narrow as well, with barely enough room to swing a sword, and only if you were a right-handed defender.

"I am not right-handed," he said, holding the sword in his left hand. "If your plan was to handicap me that way, you're shit out of luck. Are you waiting to jump as soon as I get close?"

"You're close enough," Heronimo said. There was a sound like thunder and a huge stone ball fell down the stairs.

I belched fire. It melted the nets and struck an invisible barrier. Pouring into the space, it grew feet, legs, and all the rest.

Plasma transmuted into bone. Burning bone sprouted fleshy worms. The worms twined and twisted, becoming nerves, muscles, organs. Intestines coiled out of ribbons of flame. The brain grew from a single spark. The skull was as transparent as glass.

It was beautiful. It was horrifying. The red-hot man raised his fists and screamed.

Skin appeared on his head, then flowed down the neck and shoulders like a sheet of milk. There was an explosion of steam, and then the body fell to the ground, coughing fire.

I gave a great shudder and felt myself shrink. The barbs popped out, the chains fell away, and my wounds healed over. There was an emptiness in my head—a silence not felt in weeks. I looked at Cruix and realized he was changing into a dragon. I decided I'd done enough and I blacked out.

Dinendal, broken and bleeding, lay at the bottom of the stairs. He looked up.

Heronimo hugged a huge stone to his chest. His face was knotted with the strain.

Dinendal tried to move, but couldn't. "Hey, wait a second," he said. "You're taking this kind of personal, aren't you?"

Heronimo said nothing as he came down the stairs.

"Come on, man, you're making me nervous. Come on, you can't do this! Hey! *Hey—*"

Heronimo dropped the stone on the elf's head, crushing it. Then, grunting with effort, he picked up the ball again and dropped it a second time. It made less of a crunch. Only when he kicked it aside and saw the pulpy mess beneath did he let himself sigh.

"You killed my mother. You killed my father. You killed my people. But I've killed you. Do you hear me, elf? I, Heronimo, have taken my vengeance. Our quarrel is done."

Suddenly weary, he sat down next to the body. He could hear that the battle was over.

"I could use a drink. Can't wait to raise a cold one with my friends." He looked at his stumps. "Of course, I'll need my hands first."

"Angrod?" It was Mina's voice.

"Go 'way. Sleeping."

"Master Angrod, seeing how you've won the battle, it might be good to get up and face the music."

"What, are they drumming me out of Corinthe?"

"They want a parade, actually."

I opened my eyes. Mina was bruised and bloody, but smiling. Meerwen looked happy enough, but she had her arms crossed. My uncle was beaming.

"I did just what you said, young master. I called for help and the Lord Governor teleported all the way from Drystone with a company of royal guard."

"Damn," I said. "That is major wizardry." I looked at the women. "What happened to you two?"

"This skinny elf was stuck in a hole. I had to drag her out by the ankles."

"It was a *tunnel*. The fools thought they could imprison an earth mage! I was escaping when this vulgar dwarf ruined it."

"Hey, this *vulgar* dwarf saved your life!"

"Ladies, please," I said. "Hello, Heronimo."

"Hey, Angrod," Heronimo said. "I'm getting out of the revenge business."

"Satisfied your honour, did you?"

"At some cost," he said, looking mournful. He raised his bandaged hands. "Just got them reattached. Can't seem to move them. Will I ever hold a sword again?"

"Have I ever told you that your calves lack size and definition?"

"Hey, fuck you!" he said, and made a pair of rude gestures.

"Your middle fingers work, at least."

"I—thanks."

"You'll never believe what I went through!" Mina said. Heronimo and I looked at each other.

"I just fought the greatest swordsman in Brandish. He cut off both my hands before I could kill him."

"And I chewed off my own arm so I could regurgitate an entire dragon."

I looked at my right arm, what was left of it. The stump ended just below the shoulder. "Looks like I won't be getting it back, either. But anyway, you were saying, Mina?"

She stared. "I… you guys are horrible, you know that?"

"No, no, we're totally interested in your story," Heronimo said.

"That may have to wait."

We turned and saw the Lord Governor of Drystone.

"Lord Elanesse," I said. "Have you come to arrest me?"

Like his daughter, Findecano had his arms crossed. "I thought I was. Yet you rescued Meerwen and uncovered a dangerous conspiracy. What's more, you don't seem to be the dragon we're looking for."

Cruix stepped forward. He'd been sitting so quietly I hadn't noticed, even though he was a full-grown dragon. "I take complete responsibility for any deaths I may have caused. I was disoriented after transforming for the first time, but that's no excuse." He bowed his great horned head. "I throw myself at the mercy of the court."

Anything he threw himself at would be crushed, but never mind. It was time to do my part.

"Help me up, Heronimo," I said, and climbed to my feet. "As bond-brother to the dragon Cruix, I hereby extend my protection and grant him full pardon."

"A full pardon?" Findecano said. "On whose authority?"

"On *my* authority," I said, raising my voice so it carried through the citadel. "I am the last living scion of

House Lissesul. I am friend to dwarves and humans, and kin to dragons! I believe there was a prophecy?"

"Where are your manners?" Cruix bellowed. He reared and spread his wings, framing me with his wings. *"You are in the presence of the crown prince— ANGROD VENEANAR!"*

Five hundred elves were caught in the moment and crashed to their knees. Amid the sound, I turned to Cruix.

And winked.

Epilogue

I awakened slowly, luxuriating in the feather mattress. The light from the windows told me it was close to noon, which was fine. In the royal household, the day begins when *I* get up.

I slid out of the silk sheets and scratched. Stretched. I was yawning when someone behind me said, "Prince Angrod?"

"Yaaah!" I turned and channelled fire through my arm. Then I saw it was my personal assistant. "Dagonet, don't *do* that!"

"Sorry, milord. I thought you'd be awake already."

"How did you get in? Why didn't I see you standing there?"

"It was quite a long yawn, milord. Tends to affect the hearing. And I see you'll need another sleeve."

I looked at Firescale, my silver arm. Modelled on my left arm, it felt the same and even weighed the same. Black cords of synthetic muscle tightened under the seams, everything working smoothly and soundlessly.

I flexed the fleshless fingers and grimaced. I still wasn't used to it.

"Will you be wearing the blue sleeve or the green one?"

"You know what, let's do without any sort of glove today. It's strange enough having this thing without pretending it's flesh and blood."

The arm had been a gift from Mina's father, the Chieftain of Ironore, partly for keeping his daughter safe and partly as a diplomatic gesture. I wasn't king yet, but it looked to be in the making.

"Armour-grade silver alloy, runs off an internal crystal battery," Mina had said, going over the manual. "Four-hundred-pound grip!"

"It's not going to strangle me if I go against your father, will it?"

"Of course not! Daddy never delegates. If he wanted to strangle you he'd do it himself."

Things had moved quickly from there. Valandil's pro-royalist faction had offered their support and, in light of my bargain with Cruix, I had no choice but to accept. It had taken some legal footwork, but we both had our freedom.

Auntie Marilla bustled in with the brunch trolley. Heronimo followed close behind. He was bare-chest and had a towel over his shoulders.

"Good session?" I asked.

"Very good," he said. "The fencing master says it'll only take me fourteen years to become competent."

"High praise," I said. "He's not still mad about the groin attack, is he?"

"He has forbidden it in sparring. Although I don't see the problem. It's a standard greeting among some of my people. The slower one buys the beer."

Mina came in, and this time she wore a dress. "I've just been in a meeting with the Council of Governors. You were missed. When are you going to start getting up early?"

"Get off my case, woman," I said, walking to the trolley. "It's only been weeks since the Battle of the Citadel."

"That doesn't mean you can ignore your duties. After all, you claimed them only recently."

I sighed. To keep Mina from having to return to her father I'd appointed her dwarven ambassador to my court, such as it was. She seemed to be taking it seriously.

"Here are my notes," she said. "Catch up while you eat."

I sat down on the bed and started on the bread. "I'm to officiate at a diplomatic summit, an arts festival, and a football game?"

"Several football games, actually."

"What the hell is a constitutional monarchy?"

I thought back to my carefree days in Drystone, when all I had to worry about was 'prentice work. I remembered Elrond and his fruit wines, the Merchant Quarter and its glittering nightlife. Corinthe was my home but it no longer felt like my playground.

And because everyone seemed to want to talk to me before I'd even washed my face, Cruix popped in. As an elf, he looked exactly like I did except for the hair. "Hey, bro!" he said.

"I'm not your bro. What do you want?"

"I have an excellent idea for a day trip!"

"Not now," Mina said. "Angrod has things to attend to. He's not going to have free time for a while."

Dagonet leaned close. "Meerwen's been calling. She has some things she wants to say to you."

"You see, Cruix? It's not like I don't have options."

"But this one is a group outing," he said. "Fun for the whole party!"

Mina crossed her arms. "I don't know which is more suspicious, the dragon's invitation or the Elanesse's. You can't possibly think her father doesn't know of this."

"Nice-looking lady, though," Heronimo said. "Probably fun in bed."

"Did you say something, mister?" Mina said. "Are you unhappy with our current arrangement?"

"It was just an observation," he said. "Nothing wrong with looking."

"Ha! I saw the way you were looking—"

"A man's got eyes—"

"It'd be good sport," Cruix said, "and perfect for public relations—"

"Guys, SHUT UP!"

They looked at me. I sat on the bed, a bun half-buttered in my hand. "If you're not going to let me have breakfast, at least have the decency to speak one at a time."

I gestured at Cruix. "You first. The last time I went anywhere with you, I ended up without an arm. What could you possibly say to get me out of this castle?"

"Wyvern hunting."

"I'll get my stuff."

Preview: Wyvern Hunters

Morgan stirred the cornmeal dumpling in the bowl, soaking up the last of the stew. It had been a good stew, thick with carrots and beef. He sopped it all up and ate the dumpling in one bite.

Like all good halflings, his wife never emptied the stewpot. She kept it simmering over the fire, adding what was available and dishing out what was needed. Morgan tasted hints of a hundred different meals. Beans and barley. Chicken and mutton. More than a bit of crow. He frowned, remembering recent dinners. It had been a difficult season.

"Good stew?" His wife smiled and he noted the lines around her eyes.

"It was," he said. "I hope it wasn't too expensive."

"Burke was glad to give credit, he knows you'll be back with cash."

"If Fortuna wills." He looked across the table at his son Elrick and his muleteer Volcin. They had cleaned their bowls and were pushing their chairs back.

"I'm sure we'll make lots of good trades," Elrick said. "Maybe we'll even see the elf-prince."

"Enough about the elf-prince!" Volcin was a wiry man who only smiled when you paid him. "You really think he's gonna help?"

"They say he took on an entire pack of assassins. That he chewed off his right arm to become blood brothers with a dragon."

Elrick was tall for a halfling—six feet—and thick of body and limb. He looked much like his father, except he still had his hair. "Angrod Veneanar is young," he said. "I think we'd have a lot in common."

"Young for an elf, you mean," Morgan said. "He's your grandpa's age. You remember Grandpa. No use expecting change from people that old."

Volcin snickered. "They'll want taxes, you know. He and his royal court will be just one more layer on the dungheap."

"Eww," Elrick said. "Come on. I just ate."

"And a wonderful meal it was," Morgan rumbled. He looked to his wife. "You and the girls will eat just as well, I trust?"

His wife smiled again. "We'll be fine. You need to get going."

The sun had not cleared the Northern Sea when the pack train left the village.

Algerin was home to eighteen families. The women knew a hundred ways to prepare what their husbands pulled from the sea, but man does not live on fish alone. They traded for everything else at Pithe's annual charter fair.

Morgan rode. His knees were not what they used to be. Still he kept his horse at an easy pace, partly so the men could keep up and partly because heavily-laden mules were slow to move.

Volcin had them in single file. Dried and salted cod hung from their packsaddles. A few carried barrels of cod liver oil, their most precious cargo. Nasty as the oil was, the dwarves always paid handsomely. And they paid in gold.

Morgan frowned. Quite a bit of that gold was going to Volcin and his animals. Wagons would have been cheaper but the road to Pithe was no better than a game trail. The only way to transport something was on some poor creature's back.

Elrick sidled up. "Pa, you really think Brandish won't be better with a king?"

Morgan considered it. "This being your first fair and all, you ought to focus on other things. Like maybe finding a wife."

"I thought Sarah and I would..."

"Sarah is your cousin. Your *first* cousin. Too many of the same ancestors. This ain't Mithish, boy. "

"Heh," Volcin said.

Elrick wrung his hat. "You think I'm ready?"

Morgan laughed. "Hell. I remember when I could carry you in one arm. Doesn't seem that long ago. But I can hardly do that now, can I?"

"Who would want me? Who'd want to be a fisherman's wife?"

"Some farmer's daughter? The sea would be a change of scene, at the very least."

"Don't do it, kid," Volcin said. "Marriage is a trap devised by women to keep men down."

"Listen to yourself," Morgan said. "But to answer your question, son, I don't put much faith in kings or elves. Best I can say about elves is they ignore us. And kings? Well, what is a king except a man with too much power?"

It was hard going. The road had potholes you could drown in.

There were old imperial roads that repelled water and stored up sunlight, but these were fragmentary things. They never connected to anything important. Only elves could build things like that, and these days they seldom bothered.

Morgan scanned the skies. He scanned the trees when they entered the forest. He wasn't worried about Northlander raiders. Most of the men were old like he was, the younger ones having stayed to guard the village. Dried fish and fermented oil were valuable, certainly, but humans preferred treasure that was easier to carry. No worries on the return trip either—they wouldn't be carrying much money after shopping at the fair.

No, Morgan was worried about threats of a more reptilian sort. Wyverns didn't often attack caravans this large, but you never knew.

He checked his crossbow. It was homemade, the bowstave solid wood rather than steel. Instead of a proper trigger, you squeezed a lever against the stock. Morgan would've liked to load it with a dwarven-made explosive quarrel, but those were expensive. Iron-tipped quarrels would have to do.

A crossbow was the sort of weapon you'd expect in a small coastal village. Easy to build, easy to master. Any place with a carpenter and blacksmith could turn them out and a man only needed a few lessons with them. Unlike bows, which took a lifetime to learn.

Most of the other men had crossbows, except for Jimmy, who carried an old dwarven spellgun. It was just a pistol, and it had just one charge. Jimmy had tagged along to buy bullets. Morgan suspected that dwarves sold the weapons at a loss so you'd buy overpriced ammo the rest of your life.

"What'cha thinking, Pa?"

"When we get to the fair I think I'll have me a piece of steak. A nice marbled steak with biscuits and gravy."

Volcin looked up. "Sounds good. I'll have a drink too. Haven't had decent beer in weeks. What will *you* do, kid?"

"Look for a wife, I guess? How does one do that?"

"Ask for the Wives 'r' Us auction tent. Good ones go for upward of a sov'rin. That's a hundred rupees. The really good ones have elven blood so they'll never get fat or wrinkly, but those cost at least half a yippee—five hundred rupees."

"B-but I only have twenty rupees," Elrick said. "My life savings."

"Ah, well," Volcin scratched his chin. "You'll have to settle for a buck-toothed bride with a flat chest and a tendency to nag. But I'm sure she'll grow on you."

"I don't want a buck-toothed woman!"

"You should've started saving as soon as you were born!"

Morgan laughed. "He's kidding, boy. No such thing as Wives 'r' Us. Although things would be different if this were the Northlands."

"They know how to deal with women over there," Volcin said. "I hear you can buy them fully housebroken. Well-practiced in the bedroom arts."

"And what good is that to a dog of the sea?" Morgan asked. "He'd never sail beyond sight of land for fear she'd start practicing on the neighbours. No, son. Find yourself a woman who can keep your house and bear your babies."

Volcin smirked. "Or at least a woman for whom 'We're not *too* related, are we?' isn't a pickup line."

Elrick was looking in the distance. "What if she's an elf?"

The muleskinner laughed. "An elf! Might as well ask for a princess."

"But not all elves are nobles. I know that some work for a living. What about that tinker who came by?"

Morgan remembered the tinker who'd mended the village's pots and pans. The elf hadn't used tools—he'd pass his hands over a crack and the edges would knit together. Cast iron would rust in reverse and cracked porcelain would become seamless again, thanks to his magic.

"And what about the raindancer?"

The wood elf would call down the rain, for a price. And something about the rain made plants thrive. Algerin only had vegetable gardens but the men had passed the hat anyway.

"I still don't know why you paid her, when all you got was a naked elf-woman dancing in the—oh."

"I'd have paid to see that," Volcin said.

"But seriously. An elf and me. What are the odds?"

Volcin scratched his chin. "I'll tell you at the camp."

They sat around the fire. The fog reflected the light so it seemed like they were sitting in a thundercloud.

The muleteer clipped the end of a cigar and lit it with a burning taper. He blew a smoke ring and leaned back. "This is a true story. Happened to someone I knew, a nicer guy you could not ask for. There he was, minding his own business..."

His business was overland shipping. He had two employees whose job was to carry goods to the villages where the wagons didn't run. It was steady work and it kept him outdoors. The guy thought he had everything he wanted.

"Until *she* rode into his life."

She'd been on a gray horse that first time. She wore a purple dress and a smile. Her beauty was the kind that made young men gasp and old men weep.

"She was amazing. Just amazing. Tall, even out of the saddle. Legs that went up and up. Hips you wanted to rest your hands on. A trim little waist and a bust that strained belief. A lesser woman would've had backaches."

"And her face?" Elrick leaned forward. "What about her face?"

"Her face?" Volcin puffed at his cigar, then tapped the ashes behind him. "Ah, her face."

Her hair was platinum blonde. Her eyes and lips were the colour of wine. Her face was utterly without blemish. She had three hoop earrings in one pointed ear.

"You know how elves are so perfect it's hard to tell them apart? Well, she didn't have trouble making an impression on my friend. She fixed him with a look and he knew he'd never forget her."

She said she'd been watching him. He was such a strong, handsome halfling, but she'd been too shy to introduce herself.

"Looking back, he should've suspected. Elf-men are nearly as pretty as the women. How could a weather-beaten halfling match up?"

Take me now, she said. She took his hand and led him to the trees. They made love under the shade and on the folds of her cloak.

"What was she like?" Elrick asked.

"Well," Volcin said. "She was—I mean, according to my friend, she was the best he'd ever had. If sex were an art form she'd have scholars tracing her influences. If sex were a sport she'd win all the medals. *Nothing* compared to that sweet golden pussy."

After an eternity of mating she rolled off him and they lay panting in her cloak. Then she asked him when they were going to do this again.

"It goes without saying that my friend lost interest in his business. He sold, er, let go his employees and built a cottage in the woods. His elf-woman would visit him with a basket and a lady boner. This continued for two years."

"And then what?" Elrick leaned so far forward he was almost kneeling.

"The last time he saw her, she set the cottage on fire. She gave him a bag of coins and told him never to come near her if he valued his life."

He'd been picking mushrooms when he found her in front of their love nest. He'd rushed to take her in his arms but she sneered and snapped her fingers. The house started burning. Here, she said, handing him a purse. For your time.

Volcin uncorked a jug with his teeth and took a long drink. Wine spilled down his chin and he coughed. It sounded like a sob. "The last time he saw her, it was in the city. She was with her husband, who had a brotherly resemblance with my friend. Like if one brother had been born into poverty and the other into wealth. The elves were showing off a brand-new baby."

The wyvern snaked its head around the rock and gazed at the men and mules. The three fires glowed brightly, but not so brightly it couldn't count the men. They were numerous enough to be worthwhile but not numerous enough to be a threat, not with their bee-sting weapons. It tasted the air, tasted their weariness, and knew them to be easy kills.

"She was just using your friend to get pregnant?" Elrick said. "That's harsh."

"Tell me about it." Volcin drained the jug and threw it over his shoulder. "Ah well. Plenty more fish in the sea. But I'm sure you know that."

Morgan sipped his coffee, anticipating first watch. "Fish are not women."

"Life's a woman. And all women are bitches." Volcin stood up. "Nature calls. I go to drain the elephant."

He walked off into the haze, but he hadn't gotten far when Elrick asked, "What was your friend's name?"

Volcin stopped but didn't turn. "Maybe I'm bitter. But I thought she loved me."

"He's been gone awhile, hasn't he?" Elrick asked.

It had gone quiet. Morgan turned from the fire but the glare had ruined his night vision. He brought the crossbow to his shoulder and stared into the shadows. Something rustled. "Elrick, get your back to the rock face."

"What is it, Pa?"

"I don't know. But the mules are restless."

The other men got up from their fires. Crossbows were cocked and loaded. Jimmy drew his pistol and thumbed the hammer back. Elrick squinted into the darkness. "Volcin?"

The wyvern answered.

"The elf-prince, Pa. The elf-prince!"

"Yes, yes," Morgan said. "Stay with me."

Down the road they thundered, on a single gasping horse. Morgan held the reins in one hand, his son in the other. Elrick was practically in his lap. He was very pale. "L-looks like I won't be bringing a girl home."

"Always next year, son. Stay with me." Morgan held his son tight and tried to keep him warm. The horse was sweating but the boy was much too cold.

It had happened so fast. The beast had charged into the camp, ignoring crossbow bolts and thrown harpoons. It had scattered mules and trampled men.

Jimmy was bitten in half before he could shoot. Morgan had dived after the pistol but hadn't gotten the chance to fire it.

"The elf-prince. The elf-prince!"

"Save your strength. We're almost there." He said this partly to his son, partly at the horse. Blood and froth flew from its mouth. Morgan could see the village lights through the mist.

"The elf-prince, Pa. He can help us."

"Stay with me. Stay with me." They galloped down the trail, the gray willows seeming to clutch when the horse swerved left or right. Morgan screamed for his wife. Windows and doors flew open. His wife and the girls spilled out the door. "What happened, Morgan? What—*Elrick!*"

The horse staggered to a halt. It collapsed backward and spilled them from the saddle. It kicked as it died, but Morgan ignored it. He caught up his son and ran to his wife.

"The elf-king, Pa," Elrick said. "Don't forget." And he shuddered.

"He's—he's—" The boy's mother screamed. So did his sisters. The younger one looked at her brother and wept. "His legs. What happened to his legs?"

His father had bound the stumps, but the boy had bled too fast. Morgan stared into the distance. His scalp was split and a gash ran down his back, but those hurts could not compare.

Appendix

The Races of Brandish

Halflings

Halflings, as the other races call them, are a people untouched by magic. Unlike elves, dwarves, or humans, they are unable to manipulate the arcane energies that saturate Brandish. For halflings, magic might as well not exist.

Physically they are unremarkable among the humanoid races. They're taller than dwarves but shorter than humans, stronger than elves but weaker than humans, and so on. They can be found in every major landmass. From an elven perspective they mature fast, breed explosively, and die much too young.

At this point we must discuss the interdimensional refugees. Each one arrived through a fairy ring and all of them claim to be from a world where halflings are not only the dominant species, but also the only species. If elven theories are correct, most of our world's life forms originated from this place. This includes the common ancestors of all the humanoid races. Elves, dwarves, and humans are descended from ancient halflings.

On Earth, halflings remained a single race and eventually built a civilization that covered the planet. On Brandish, while halflings are the most populous people, they remain a political minority. Halfling settlements are found virtually everywhere and halflings are abundant in every city, even the elven capital. Nevertheless, they remain marginalized for several reasons. They are scattered and disunited. They lack any sort of cohesive identity or culture. They are therefore second-class citizens.

If halflings were to rally together, they could grow into a mighty power. The interdimensional refugees prove that they are capable enough. Their short lifespans mean that their culture can change much faster than any other, and while they lack magic, they have no trouble using magical tools and weapons. There's also the weight of their numbers. They outnumber everybody.

Humans

If halflings are only the most recent wave of humanoids, humans must be the second most recent. Apart from their greater size and robustness, what sets them apart from halflings is their gift of regeneration. This allows them to recover from wounds that would kill or cripple others. It's one reason their society is so violent.

A human can survive massive amounts of trauma. Maim them, gut them, flay them alive and they will recover if allowed. Missing parts will grow back. Their limbs can be reattached, even swapped. They feel pain, but don't go into shock. About the only things that will slow their healing are fire, poison, and starvation. About the only things that will kill a human are decapitation and severe blood loss.

Because casual violence is largely consequence-free for humans, their sports are extremely rough. Even their children games are more like brawls. As a result, each human is a formidable combatant and can be expected to participate in any fight. Every man, woman, and child may be considered a legitimate military target.

While humans exist in every land, the heart of their civilization (such as it is) can be found in the Northlands. Humans are farmers, fishermen, and traders, but above all they are rovers, raiders, and reavers—their history is a tapestry of piracy and war. They never developed beyond chiefdoms and tribes. Their economic theories are, frankly, barbaric. While others believe in honest labour and fair trade, they believe in accumulating treasure and chattel. Their towns and cities run on halfling slave labour.

Humans would be a greater threat if they weren't so divided. Individually they are superb warriors. A unified human force is the stuff of nightmares.

Dwarves

Dwarves are short, squat, and bearded, or at least the men are bearded. To outsiders they present a serious face, seeming to be as solid and as stolid as the mountains they call home. Once you get to know them, though, you find they have as much emotional range as anyone. Dwarves have a sense of humour. It tends to be a grim one, though.

Pound for pound, they are the strongest of the manlike races, with thick, heavy bodies that are capable of great endurance. Their outsized hands are amazing for delicate work as well. Coupled with the ability to 'see' magical effects, this makes them master artificers. Other races can imbue things with power, but only dwarves are able to craft things that work constantly, consistently, and at a high level.

Given enough time, it is possible for a dwarf to replicate most elven spells, but for safety reasons their goods usually carry low-level enchantments. The effects are normally impossible to adjust as well. Dwarves can only manipulate magic through their tools, which puts them at a disadvantage in terms of power and precision. On the other hand, anyone can use their devices, even halflings. A spellgun will always fire, no matter who pulls the trigger.

Dwarves are always ready to trade. They are confined to their mountain cities and underground towns by law, and there are many things they cannot produce themselves. Dwarves will accept fish, fruit, grain, and other foodstuffs. They will also take raw fabric, unprocessed ore, and rough lumber. Their forges hunger for charcoal and their palates thirst for beer. It isn't hard to find something they would gladly pay for.

While still active in the world, dwarf populations haven't grown in centuries. This may be related to the epidemic of low fertility among elves. Then again, dwarves may simply be having trouble expanding underground. They were made to live on the surface, after all.

Elves

Elves are beautiful and cruel. Elves are powerful and eternal. You hear this often, mostly from the other races. While the eternal part is exaggerated, elves have certainly proven their power and cruelty many times. When dealing with other races they are not known for their tolerance or restraint.

Elves are descended from the first people to arrive in Brandish. Physically they aren't much different from halflings. From an outside viewpoint, elven men are more pretty than handsome and elven women are universally beautiful, if hard to tell apart. Elves are a little shorter and lighter, their features are a bit more angular, and their eyes are somewhat bigger. Nevertheless, elves and halflings could pass for each other if it wasn't for the pointy ears.

Of course, elves do not simply look different. Their facility with magic is their chief advantage. What does an elf care if an opponent is bigger than she is, when internalized magic can make her faster and stronger? What does an elf care how many his foes are, when he can incinerate them with a thought? All elves know magic. Only the sons of the wealthy become wizards, but few elves are so poor as to grow up without a trade. Artisans use trade-specific spells, women know cleaning and cooking spells, and even unskilled labourers have heavy-lifting magic.

Only a select few are taught combat magic. This is supposedly to keep dangerous criminals from becoming even more dangerous but it mainly serves to keep power in the hands of the right people—the landed aristocracy. The elves could have many more combat mages if they taught everyone who could learn.

Aside from spellcasters, elves also have the Royal Guard, a small but powerful military. Well-drilled and well-equipped, each soldier is a master martial artist and minor magician. Confident in their innate superiority as elves and warriors, royal guardsmen will face overwhelming numbers. They usually win.

Massive magical superiority, fast and hard-hitting troops, and the ability to teleport around the battlefield —it's easy to see why elves dominate the world. Nevertheless, signs indicate that they have been in decline for generations. Their numbers dwindle. Their society has turned inward. It seems inevitable that their rule will be challenged.

Caprans

Little is known about this race of goat-people. Caprans do not actually live in Brandish: they only visit from the neighbouring dimension known as the Silver World. An entire race of tourists, if you will.

Caprans are nearly as strong and as hardy as dwarves and humans. They have refined palates but claim to be able to eat almost anything. They are cheerful and delight in good food, strong drink, and pleasant company. A capran is usually the life of a party, although they must have a serious side somewhere or they would never have developed a civilization.

Besides elves, caprans are the only humanoid species to use magic directly. Their spellcasting is erratic, however. Even an experienced capran sorcerer has no way to tell exactly what a spell will do. It could be twice as strong, or a tenth as strong. It could be delayed or even reversed. This makes combat magic extremely unpredictable for them and it's likely that caprans don't field combat mages the way elves do.

Caprans do have an invaluable talent, and that is the ability to brew potions. They take in energy and bind it to an elixir, essentially creating liquid spells. As far as we know, there are no limits to this—capran potions can do anything that elven spells can.

The tactical value of potions lies in their ability to be prepared beforehand. A potioneer can thus eliminate much of the unpredictability of capran magic, although it may take several tries to get exactly the right mix.

Magic potions, like enchanted items, can be used by anyone. There is thus a brisk trade between our world and the capran world.

Our information on the Silver World is not as detailed as we would like. What is certain is that capran activity in our world is steadily increasing. Whether this is leading to anything remains to be seen.

The Cities of Brandish

Halflings from Earth have commented on the size and complexity of elven cities. In contrast to the medieval backwardness of Brandish's countryside, its metropolitan areas are clean, orderly, and heavily-populated. Most cities are home to tens of millions, making them as large and as well-developed as any city from that other world.

Elves like to have four of everything. Unsurprisingly, their settlements are made up of four distinct areas. Each is a city in itself.

The **Old Quarter** is naturally the oldest part of the city. It is usually encircled by walls and towers, and since many elven cities originally belonged to the dwarves, the buildings here may be considerably different, with early elven architecture resting on dwarven foundations. The city guard is based here, and much of the common folk live here as well. Cheap lodging can usually be found among the tenements and apartment buildings.

The **Palace Quarter** is generally the second-oldest part of the city. Standing prominently apart from the Old Quarter, it is established when a city becomes large enough that the nobility can live apart from the commoners. First a citadel for the royal guard is built, then a palace for the king or city governor. The homes of the rich follow and the rest of the space is taken up by parks. As the Palace Quarter is the local seat of government, it is often fortified as well.

The **Merchant Quarter** grows out of the interaction between the Old Quarter and the Palace Quarter. People find it convenient for businesses to have their own districts as the city grows. The Merchant Quarter is home to middle-class tradesmen, who reside in the same buildings where they work. Much of the city's entertainment can also be found in this quarter. During the day there are streets lined with restaurants and shops, and during the night there are bars, dance halls, and other establishments that never close. Most mage's citadels are here for those reasons.

The **Manufacturing Quarter** is the last part of the city to take shape. Set as close as possible to the trade routes, this section is full of warehouses and stockyards. There are also slaughterhouses, tanneries, and alchemical workshops. Any industry too noisy or smelly for the other areas will find itself in the Manufacturing Quarter.

DRYSTONE • City of Glass

The current elven capital is actually the newest city in Brandish, having been founded only four thousand years ago. Originally a scattering of fishing villages on either side of the Kingsriver, Drystone saw heavy development during the Age of Expansion.

While the ocean-spanning Elven Empire is now but a memory, the fortified harbour remains. This jetty and defensive wall was built using the drystone technique, hence the name. Massive stones were piled atop one other without mortar, their sides fitted so that no wave or tremor could loosen them. A more conventional rampart was built on this foundation once it cleared sea level—once the stones were *raised high and made dry*, as the song goes. The ultra-hard protective glass coating (a local specialty) was added later.

The tall ships no longer sail to the Fourth Continent but the extensive infrastructure ensures Drystone's pre-eminence in shipbuilding and trade. With access to both Kings Lake and the sea, the city can send cargoes directly to Lamemheth, Corinthe, Deepwood, Vergath, as well as to the Northlands. Trade with Pithe and Mithish is less simple, but the overland routes are still shorter thanks to the lake.

Drystone's status as a commercial hub makes it one of the richest and most culturally diverse cities. It may not be as steeped in history but you can buy or enjoy almost anything in this glittering city by the sea.

LAMEMHETH • City of Second Chances

The Goldore Mountains hold the largest gold deposits in Brandish. There are also considerable quantities of silver, and the two metals are often alloyed together. The dwarves control most of the underground mines. However, even a surface prospector can pan enough gold dust to make a decent living, or occasionally have an indecent amount of fun.

Lamemheth is good at catering to the suddenly wealthy. A crystal dome ensures it's always happy hour, there are more casinos and hotels than in the rest of the realm, and the entire Merchant Quarter is a red-light district. Most things are for sale in Lamemheth—little is forbidden in Brandish's entertainment capital.

Mining and tourism are the city's mainstays but it also trades in fine woods and furs. The former come from the surrounding forests, which are full of rock elms and other timber, while the latter come from the Northlands. Human traders prefer Lamemheth to Drystone.

Although the city has a Great House, it has no Lord Governor. Instead, a council of prominent citizens dictate policy to an appointed manager. The arrangement works well despite most of the council members having ties to organized crime.

Lamemhessians are ethnically diverse. Not only are there more dwarfs, humans, halflings, and caprans living in one place, but the local society is much more tolerant of multiracial people. Exotic combinations are a natural by-product of the city's sex trade.

PITHE • Elven Bread Basket

Shielded from the north wind by the Ironore Mountains, Pithe enjoys better weather than Corinthe, its closest neighbour. Together with its proximity to fertile plains and to Pithe Lake, the largest freshwater reservoir in Brandish, the city is in a position to supply food to the entire realm.

The area is so important that the elven kings ruled it with a gentle hand. Pithe's local government enjoys lighter taxes and more autonomy than any other. However, the kings also ensured that the city would never secede—it lacks modern fortifications but hosts a large royal garrison.

The Age of Expansion saw the construction of a canal linking Pithe Lake with Kings Lake. Much of Brandish's grain passes through Pithe Canal, making it a vital part of the kingdom.

Pitheans aren't especially cosmopolitan or ethnically diverse, but they are cheerful and hardworking. Jaded Drystonians might find the nightlife dull. The cuisine is a delight, though.

CORINTHE • Fortress of the North

Despite its easy access to resources and to the sea, Corinthe is known for its martial tradition. Harsh winters and centuries of conflict have produced a tough people. Living so far from other elven settlement tends to breed stoicism, and Corinthans have dealt ruthlessly with dragon attack or barbarian raid.

Surprisingly for a city that sees so much violence, Corinthe is only lightly fortified. It lacks an encircling wall, which in any case would have been useless against dragons. Instead it relies on watchtowers to warn its militia.

The city is known for its ice wines and alchemical products. However, Corinth's chief export has always been fighting men. Its citizens make enduring troops, and House Veneanar has traditionally supplied the Royal Guard with its best officers.

Corinthe's fortunes have declined somewhat since the fall of empire. The demand for soldiers and administrators is not what it once was. The winters are still as unrelenting as ever, however, and so Corinthans endure.

MITHISH • Old Eastern Capital

The Dwarven Wars are twenty millennia past, but traces of that conflict are still clear upon the landscape. As their names suggest, Pithe and Mithish were originally dwarven settlements before they were occupied by elven armies. They became forward bases from which the elves could strike at the Ironore Mountains. Later they denied access to farmland.

Not only was Mithish the first settlement to be captured, but it was also the one to block the dwarves from the sea. It therefore carried great strategic importance. It gained even more importance when the first elven dynasty made Mithish its capital. As a result, the city was almost constantly under siege. It is a fortress city even today—loyal troops still man walls that would be a familiar sight to the earliest kings.

Mithish retains a martial tradition second only to Corinthe's. Mithenians consider themselves superior to anyone else and are more than willing to prove it on the battlefield. More royal guard recruits come from Mithish than from any other city. So numerous are they, in fact, that their remittances are one of two things supporting Mithish's economy.

The city has never produced enough trade surpluses, despite adequate resources. Its local industries are a joke. The second thing keeping its economy afloat are the tariffs imposed on all imports and exports. Since Mithish sits astride the trade routes to and from the Ironore Mountains, it controls the flow of goods that goes both ways. The dwarves are doubly taxed—once when they import food and raw materials and again when they export finished products. The profits are enormous. The Mithenian nobility is known for its extravagant lifestyle.

DEEPWOOD • Elven Sanctuary

Most elves consider themselves sophisticated and modern. That's why they live in their grand cities and ignore the countryside. It wasn't always like this, though. While the dwarves were carving their fortresses in the mountains, the elves were struggling in the forests. Deepwood was where they nearly went extinct.

Dragons dominated the land. The humanoids were few, and they tried not to be noticed. Unfortunately, the terrible reptiles noticed that the elves were growing powerful in magic. This began a war of extermination. Every forest burned except for Deepwood, which wasn't simply a collection of trees—it was all the trees, an island-spanning superorganism with a single root system. It had more than enough magic to defend itself from dragons.

It took centuries, but eventually the siege lifted. Elves once again ventured into the world. Over the millennia they became powerful enough to battle dragons on equal terms. An uneasy peace followed. Hostilities were forgotten as the dragons died out and the elves entered their own period of decline.

This is ancient history, but some elves still remember. Almost all of them live in Deepwood, enough to make it the seventh most populous elven settlement. They are dedicated to preserving the old ways and protecting the forest's secrets.

VERGATH • Strange Southern City

Vergath, on the southernmost end of Brandish, is unusual even by elven standards. Founded after the Dragon Wars by a council of wizards, the city has long been the foremost centre of magical learning. It is a favoured destination for student wizards and home to many of the best minds in Brandish.

Rising high above the Green Plain, Vergath Citadel utterly dominates the rest of the city. Its four massive towers don't even try to harmonize with the natural surroundings. Each gilded spire holds libraries and laboratories where master mages advance the state of the art.

Since the city has no other industries of note except ranching, it can be considered an oversized college town. There is enough farming and fishing that Vergath is entirely self-sufficient in food, however. This has always made the elven kings nervous. The magocracy say that they have no plans for independence, but their well-trained mercenary army says different.

Politics aside, Vergath is worth visiting for its architecture and cuisine. What's more, the city is constantly pioneering new movements in art, music, and religion. Tourists are sure to enjoy the many subcultures as long as they remember that not all of the groups are peace-loving or sane.

About the Author

KLAY TESTAMARK is a man with many interests. He's sold luxury cars, created mobile apps, and exported designer clothing. Before that he was a bouncer, bodyguard, and bartender. Nowadays he's proud to be a husband and father—he and his family divide their time between Las Vegas and the Caribbean. Klay has recently returned to his first love, fantasy fiction, and *Stone Dragon* is the first of a twelve-part series. Connect with him through @klaytestamark on Twitter and visit klaytime.com.

Would you like to know when the next book is out?
Email **Klay@Klaytime.com** with the subject *Mailing List*. You can also contact him through **twitter.com/klaytestamark** and **facebook.com/klaytestamark**